SAPPHIRE IN THE SAND

Emma is sixteen years old and in love with Andrew, but he's engaged to Julie, Emma's beautiful elder sister. When their two families go to France on holiday together Emma is perturbed by Julie's casual attitude to the engagement and her interest in Yves Courtelle, another guest at the hotel. Emotions become hopelessly entangled, and for the four young people, the holiday threatens to end in tragedy as they struggle with feelings which are stronger than they are.

Books by Patricia Robins
in the Linford Romance Library:

THE FOOLISH HEART

PATRICIA ROBINS

SAPPHIRE IN THE SAND

Complete and Unabridged

LINFORD
Leicester

First published in Great Britain in 1967

First Linford Edition
published 2008

British Library CIP Data

Robins, Patricia
    Sapphire in the sand.—Large print ed.—
    Linford romance library
    1. Love stories
    2. Large type books
    I. Title
    813.5′4 [F]

    ISBN 978–1–84782–416–5

Published by
F. A. Thorpe (Publishing)
Anstey, Leicestershire

Set by Words & Graphics Ltd.
Anstey, Leicestershire
Printed and bound in Great Britain by
T. J. International Ltd., Padstow, Cornwall

This book is printed on acid-free paper

1

Emma had never been happier. It wasn't just ordinary happiness. It was breathless delight; a feeling that life was taking on a new dimension, all gold and radiant with joy.

She looked across the crowded room eagerly and saw Andrew talking to her father. She wondered what they were saying to one another; hoped Father wouldn't keep Andrew too long. He'd promised to have another dance with her.

Her heart melted. Being in love was wonderful, beautiful, exciting. Impossible to say when she had fallen in love with Andrew but she knew the exact moment she'd realised it was true — half an hour ago when Andrew had kissed her softly and told her she looked fabulous and this was the best evening of his life.

Now it seemed as if she must always

have loved him. There was never a time she had not known him for their houses adjoined and the two families were close friends as well as neighbours, the children constantly in and out of both gardens as if they were just one big one.

Andrew was the only boy in his household although he had two sisters. Marie was married now and Andrew came next — twenty-two, with Lindy, his younger sister, the same age as Emma — sixteen.

Emma had no older brothers. Julie was the eldest in her family and she was twenty-one tonight. This was her party. Emma adored Julia who was gay, extroverted, fun to be with and very attractive, too. She tried to model herself on her sister, but somehow it never really worked out. She remained Julie's opposite — small, dark, shy and rather plain. At least, she had always thought she was plain until tonight. But if Andrew thought she looked fab, then she could think so, too.

Emma felt she must get away from

the crowd of guests — be alone for a little while to savour this new strange feeling of being in love.

She slipped out of the room and went to sit on the stairs where it was cooler and the light only dim. Her cheeks were burning as if she'd caught the sun.

'Pst! Emma!'

It was Paul, her ten-year-old brother with Penny, aged eight. Too young to be allowed to stay up for Julie's party, they'd nevertheless been secretly enjoying it from the top landing. Paul, in red and blue striped pyjamas and Penny in her blue nylon nightie, looked very young and Emma wanted to hug them both. She wanted them to be as happy as she was. She said:

'Shall I sneak you up something to eat?'

'Golly! Thanks!'

Emma slipped downstairs to the dining room where the remains of the buffet supper lay on the table. She found cold chicken and cheese straws, trifle and potato salad. Giggling, she took two heaped plates upstairs to the waiting children, hoping it wouldn't make them sick.

'What's everyone *doing*?' Penny asked between mouthfuls. 'What presents did Julie get?'

Emma answered all their questions. Only as she listed Julie's birthday gifts did she realise that Andrew had come empty-handed. But she forgot a moment later as she heard her father's voice, making some kind of announcement.

'What's happening?' Penny asked impatiently. Penny was really a smaller edition of Julie — bright, intelligent, alert and always eager to be in on everything. She had the same fair hair and startlingly blue eyes. Paul was more like her, Emma, small for his age, dark haired and with shy, dark eyes.

'If you shut up, Penny, I might be able to hear,' she said. But the voice was muffled and Emma couldn't make out the words.

'Probably Daddy's proposing a toast to Julie,' she said. As if to endorse her guess, everyone began clapping. Voices were raised in a cheer and there was a lot of laughter — glasses clinking.

'I'd better go back!' Emma said. 'And you two had better go to bed; it must be midnight. I'll come and tell you what it's all about in a minute or two.'

She waited a moment longer while the children wandered along the passage towards their bedroom. Downstairs someone had put on a record.

'I'll miss my dance with Andrew!' she thought, suddenly wanting to be back with everyone, part of the fun and excitement. Above all she wanted to be near Andrew.

'Andrew's a lucky chap . . . '

'They'll make a fine couple . . . '

Two of the guests had come out of the drawing room into the hall. Emma stood looking down at them, her forehead creased in thought. What did they mean? Why was Andrew lucky?

'Oh, Emma — you didn't miss the announcement, did you?'

'I was having a chat with Paul and Penny.'

'My dear child — what a moment to choose. But perhaps you knew already?'

'Knew? Knew what?' The words came out with difficulty, choking in her throat as she steadied herself with a hand on the banisters.

'About Andrew and Julie getting engaged. Isn't it marvellous! Of course, it's just what your parents hoped for and Andrew's parents, too. So romantic, I always think, when childhood sweethearts decide to get married.'

Somehow Emma managed to excuse herself with a smile, to get away from them. Never, never again, she thought passionately, would she like Mr. and Mrs. Albright. For the rest of her life she would remember them as the couple who broke her heart.

Julie nearly collided with her in the drawing room doorway. She was wearing a turquoise-blue shift dress which accentuated the blue eyes, outlined a sooty black — the colour of the lashes. Her eyes looked enormous and sparkled with excitement.

'So there you are, Emma. Aren't you going to congratulate me, darling! Look — look, Emma, at my ring!'

She held out her hand. On the third finger shone a blue sapphire engagement ring.

'Andrew's present to me!' she laughed and impulsively hugged Emma to her.

'I — I didn't know — I never realised . . . ' Emma broke off, unable to trust her voice.

Julie laughed again.

'Of course you didn't. I didn't know, either — not until tonight. Isn't it strange, Emma, everyone always expected Andrew and me to fall in love and we never did. Then when the families had just about given up hoping, suddenly it happened — just like that! Andrew says he's always been in love with me but he kept it a deep dark secret because he knew I didn't feel the same way.'

'But now you do?'

'Of course I do, Emma. I suppose it is all a bit mad — the way it happened — just suddenly in the middle of a dance. Andrew said: 'I'm in love with you, Julie. Will you marry me?' Well, I thought he was joking until I looked at him and then suddenly something went ping inside me and my heart sort of stopped beating and I knew I was in love . . . with him. Isn't it marvellous?'

'Fab!' Emma said. 'I — I think your ring is lovely.'

Julie seemed not to notice the strained words. She looked at the ring and sighed:

'Just think, Emma, I'm really and truly engaged. Oh, it's so exciting. I'm going up to tell the children — I'm sure they're awake. See you later, Emma.'

Emma felt the floor swaying — made a supreme effort and let go of the banisters. She wanted to run away, to lock herself in her bedroom and cry and cry — cry all the pain out of her broken heart. But she couldn't — not now or later. No one must ever guess that she'd been silly enough, juvenile enough, to believe Andrew loved her just because he'd kissed her on the cheek and told her she looked pretty.

'I can't bear it!' she thought, but she knew she must; knew she had to go and find Andrew, smile at him, congratulate him.

'Emma!' He swept her up into his arms and hugged her. 'Are you pleased? I do hope so. You'll be my sister-in-law soon. Isn't it wonderful? You and Lindy always said you wished you were sisters and now you will be. Oh, I'm so *happy*, Emma. I never believed Julie would say yes.'

'But you bought the ring . . . '

Andrew laughed, his brown eyes crinkling in a way which had always attracted her.

'Oh, a kind of desperate belief that if I had the ring Julie would know I was serious and take me seriously. She never has done that before — as you well know, Emma.'

He tucked her arm in his and led her into the dining room where absent-mindedly, he began to eat. Watching him, Emma wondered how it was

9

possible for a human heart to break and yet not show.

'Aren't you hungry, Emma? I'm ravenous. Just think, Emma, Julie loves me. I still can't quite believe it, can you? I'm really such a dull ordinary chap and she — she's so pretty, so attractive. Yet she loves me — she said so. I can't believe my good luck.'

Suddenly Emma felt his doubt communicate itself to her. Did Julie love Andrew? Really love him? Snatches of conversation flooded her mind now — sisterly discussions they'd had in the privacy of their bedroom.

'Andrew kissed me this afternoon behind the beech tree . . . ' Julie's infectious laugh. 'I quite liked it but somehow it wasn't in the least romantic. Trouble is, I know Andrew too well — far too well. He'll always seem like a brother to me, Emma. He was awfully cross with me because I laughed. I suppose I was awful. Boys hate it if you don't take them seriously.'

How long ago had Julie said those

words — a week — a month at most. What had changed her suddenly — or changed her attitude to Andrew? If Julie had been falling in love with him, she'd have told Emma. Julie was immensely extroverted and she discussed all her boy friends with Emma in the greatest detail. Julie had a sharp critical mind and Emma had sometimes wondered if her sister would ever find a boy without something about him she had to criticise. Now, it seemed, she had suddenly decided Andrew was everything she wanted. It didn't make sense — didn't ring true.

A crowd of guests including Andrew's parents came into the dining room looking for him. They gathered round expressing renewed delight at his engagement, turning to Emma to include her in their pleasure so that she was forced to smile; to say how wonderful it was. It was a full five minutes before she could escape. She ran upstairs to the large sunny bedroom she shared with Julie and only then did she give way to tears.

But she could not give herself up to the luxury of a good cry. Mother was far too observant and would want to know the cause of swollen red-rimmed eyes. So, too, would Julie. Anxiously, Emma sprang off the bed and dashed ice-cold water from the basin over her flushed face and pricking eyes.

'I look a sight!' she thought. The shelf above the basin was littered with Julie's make-up. Julie was frantically untidy and couldn't get ready for a party without leaving the room looking as if a hurricane had been through it. Carefully and methodically, Emma began to put things away. Once she stopped to put on a light dusting of powder over her shining nose and an even lighter touch of lipstick. Mother wasn't keen on her wearing a lot of makeup — not until she was seventeen which would be in a few months time.

'Oh,' thought Emma tremulously. 'Sixteen is an awful age to be — neither young nor grown up!' Surely, she told herself, one's life couldn't really be over at sixteen. Yet what hope was there for her now? She'd lost the only boy she could ever love — and lost him to her adored sister so that she could not even have the luxury of hoping something would go wrong with the engagement so that Andrew turned to her in the end.

Julie could be as exasperating as any older sister but she was far more lovable than hatable! She lent Emma her nylons, let her practise with her make-up; spent hours washing and setting Emma's dark hair, trying to find a becoming style for it that was also fashionable *and* acceptable to Mother. Many was the time Julie had taken the blame for something because she knew Emma dreaded Mother's serious disapproving moods whereas Julie took little notice of them, saying Mother would soon get over it. Julie had helped enormously with O levels last year and now while she, Emma, was studying for her A's, Julie was just as helpful. Emma wouldn't have blamed her if having swotted through her own exams and finished for ever with school, she had refused to think in terms of logarithms and Latin translations again.

No, Emma told herself as she folded Julie's blue jeans over a hanger and put them in the wardrobe, she would never do anything to make Julie unhappy. If only she could believe that she really did love Andrew. Andrew was like a brother to them all. He was just part of the family.

Emma sighed. It wasn't, of course, true. If she herself had had secret dreams, written in her locked five-year diary, about her adoration for him, so might Julie have done the same. Maybe Julie had been in love with him for *ages* and just hadn't told Emma about it for fear of family teasing.

She went to the white painted desk in the corner of the room and took out her diary, unlocking it with the tiny key she wore on a silver chain round her neck. Leafing back a few pages she read:

The day after tomorrow is Julie's

party. Can't wait. Have a new red dress
— fab. Hope Andrew likes it. It makes
me look at least eighteen. Hope
Andrew dances with me. Saw him
yesterday and he's coming to tennis this
afternoon . . . .

Of course, she thought as she put the
diary away, unable to bear the sight of
those lost hopes, she hadn't known
until tonight that she was actually in
love with Andrew. That knowledge had
come as a certainty when he kissed
her. What a little fool she had been
imagining it was a real kiss. Not that
she'd anything to compare it with but
she'd read in books what real kissing
was and Andrew's peck on the cheek
couldn't possibly have been mistaken
for a lover's kiss. All the same, her heart
had turned over and at that moment,
she had known she loved him. Was this
what had happened to Julie, too? Had
Andrew suddenly kissed her and Julie
realised that she'd really loved him all
along?

Emma went across to the window

and drew back the curtains. The garden was flooded with moonlight — a night for lovers, for romance, for dreams. Perhaps somewhere in the garden, Julie and Andrew were walking hand in hand, standing with their arms around one another . . .

She felt sick with jealousy and with hatred at her own thoughts. Somehow she must try to start thinking of Andrew as a brother-in-law, as Julie's future husband. But at present, it just did not seem possible. Maybe if he'd been a stranger it would be easier. But the years of growing-up had happened so gradually, she'd never thought of Andrew as old enough to get married — or Julie. She'd never thought of Julie getting engaged, married. Julie was so unpredictable and especially about her boy friends. She had dozens and it was never the same boy two weeks' running. No one in the family took her affairs in the least seriously. Father would come down to breakfast in the mornings and invariably he'd ask Julie who was today's lover-boy. Julie was in and out of love as often as a honey bee was in and out of different flowers. Now, suddenly, she was engaged.

'Emma! Darling, what on earth are you doing, tidying up at this hour. Everyone's going. Crazy girl. Come down at once and say goodbye!'

Julie caught her young sister round the waist and twirled her around excitedly. Her face was flushed and her eyes brilliant. Emma had never seen her more beautiful.

'Oh, I'm so happy!' Julie said. 'Isn't life wonderful, Emma? Isn't my ring just gorgeous? Isn't Andrew a dream?' She dragged Emma out of the room and downstairs where people where already putting on coats and preparing to go. Andrew was the last to leave.

'Come and see me off, darling!' he said to Julie, but of course, as he was only going into the next-door garden, Emma and her mother and father knew that he just wanted a moment alone with her to kiss her goodnight.

Emma followed her mother into the kitchen.

Mrs. Prescott looked flushed and happy.

'Isn't it wonderful, Emma?' she beamed. 'All these years your father and I have been hoping one day Julie and Andrew would fall in love and now it's happened. Andrew's parents are as thrilled as we are. They really are a perfect match. Julie's so harum-scarum and Andrew's a sensible, thoughtful boy — he'll be able to put a brake on her, keep her in order.'

Father chuckled.

'He'll have a job on his hands and no mistake.' He put an arm round Emma's shoulders and hugged her. 'Now, my Emma would make a far better wife than Julie ever will. Reckon Andrew should have waited a year or two and chosen you, eh, Poppet?'

Emma gulped. Father was trying to be nice to her, afraid she might be feeling out of things; wanting to let her know Julie wasn't going to have all the compliments, but he couldn't have chosen a worse way to show his love. *If Andrew had waited . . .*

'Up to bed, Emma!' Mother said with a sudden sharp look at the dark circles under Emma's eyes. 'You look exhausted. And there's to be no gossiping all night with Julie.' Her voice softened as she bent her cheek to receive Emma's kiss. 'It seems only yesterday Julie was wearing a gym tunic and school blazer and studying for her exams.' She sighed: 'Next thing it'll be you, Emma — though not for a year or two yet, thank goodness. At least I've still one schoolgirl to fuss over.'

'Schoolgirl!' Emma thought bitterly as she went slowly upstairs to bed. 'If that's how Mother thinks of me, probably Andrew does, too. They don't know that inside me I am grown-up — old enough to know what it's like being in love; how much it hurts!'

She undressed and washed, brushed her hair and climbed into bed. With the light off, the moonlight came flooding back into the room, cold, mysterious, unfriendly. And somewhere out in the night, Andrew was kissing Julie good-night.

'I won't think about it, I won't!' she cried, burying her face in her pillow.

When Julie came up to bed a quarter of an hour later, Emma pretended to be asleep, for she knew that if Julie so much as mentioned Andrew's name, she would no longer be able to control the rush of tears.

2

'I think it's just wonderful you and I will be sisters by marriage!' Lindy's voice was muffled because the two girls were lying face down on the sand, their heads on their arms.

'That's one good thing about it!' Emma said incautiously.

Lindy's round, freckled face twisted round to look at her friend anxiously.

'Oh, Emma, don't you think the engagement is a good thing, either? I thought your family were so pleased!'

The two girls were enjoying the second day of their joint family holiday in Brittany. The families had often shared summer holidays but this was the first time they had all been abroad together. They were staying in a small hotel almost on the jetty of the little fishing village of Île Tudy. Between them they took up most of the bedrooms and there were only two other families in the hotel, both French. At their own request, Emma and Lindy were sharing a bedroom. As a rule Emma shared with Julie but this time she had asked to change the usual arrangement. Julie wanted to discuss Andrew whenever she and Emma were alone and Emma felt she couldn't cope with her sister's confidences — at least not until she had become more used to the idea of Andrew as her future brother-in-law.

At the moment the two younger children were fishing for crabs on the rocks of the beach at St. Marine. Emma and Lindy were in charge. Julie had gone sailing with Andrew and would drive to St. Marine later in the afternoon to take them all back to the hotel.

Emma sat up, hunching her knees and glancing across the beach to check on the children. They both wore bathing suits for the August sunshine was wonderfully hot. Presently, when they had finished crabbing, they would swim; she and Lindy, too.

It would all be so perfect if it were not for her private worries about Julie and Andrew. Now it seemed as if Lindy, too, was worried.

'Mother and Father are madly enthusiastic!' Lindy was saying as she picked up a handful of sand and let it run out slowly through her fingers. 'But I don't think Andrew's all that happy. He was that first week but since then he's looked sort of worried and pre-occupied, as if he's got something on his mind. You do think Julie really loves him, don't you?'

Not even to Lindy, her very best friend, could Emma bring herself to be disloyal to Julie. Besides, she was far too unsure of her understanding of the situation. She doubted whether Julie was a hundred per cent in love with Andrew but knew her suspicions could be wishful thinking and hated herself for having them.

'I just don't know!' she said thoughtfully. 'What do you think?'

Lindy sighed.

'Well, they had a ghastly quarrel the evening before we left home — Wednesday I suppose it was. I was watching television and they were next door in the dining room. Andrew was upset because Julie had been to the cinema with Anthony Bains. I suppose I shouldn't have listened, but they were both shouting so I couldn't help it. Andrew said Julie shouldn't go out with any other boy now she was engaged to him and Julie said she wasn't going to be a prisoner and Andrew was being old-fashioned and ought to trust her. Of course, they made it up and they seem all right since we came out here.'

Emma looked at Lindy doubtfully. She knew Julie had been to a film with Anthony — a tall, thin boy with glasses who worked in the County Library. Andrew really had no cause to be jealous of Anthony and yet Emma couldn't understand why Julie wanted to go out with anyone but Andrew.

'Well, I want to see the film, you silly

goose!' Julie had explained at the time. 'And you won't be back from your shopping in London and Andrew's playing golf, so who else can I go with?'

Anthony was known in the family as 'the old faithful'. He could always be rung up at the last moment to make up numbers; always turned up at the eleventh hour when an extra boy was needed. He didn't seem to mind being 'used' and they all took him for granted. Andrew knew that very well. It was silly to quarrel over him. But then Julie and Andrew had always quarrelled violently. Usually over nothing more important than the tennis score or the height of the highest mountain in the world or something equally inconsequential. Andrew argued coolly and logically, Julie heatedly and irrationally. In the end, Julie would suddenly capitulate and burst out laughing and the whole incident would be forgotten. That was one of the nicest things about Julie — she never sulked even when she lost the argument. So maybe she and

Andrew would go on quarrelling in just the same way after they were married and it wouldn't matter.

Lindy said:

'Julie's so pretty, I don't wonder Andrew is jealous. Did you notice that French boy in the hotel at dinner last night? He was staring at Julie all the time.'

'No, I didn't see!' Emma replied. But she knew to whom Lindy referred because, although she had her back to the French family at the adjoining table, Paul and Penny sat opposite and behaved disgracefully, giggling and whispering because they said the French boy was staring.

'I think he's very nice looking,' Lindy went on. 'He's got brown wavy hair and dark brown eyes and he's terribly tanned. He isn't as tall as Andrew but I should think he's about the same age.'

Emma sighed.

'I wish I was much older or much younger!' she said. 'I don't like being sixteen at all, do you, Lindy?'

Lindy laughed.

'I don't mind. I wouldn't want to be younger, anyway. I wouldn't mind being Julie's age and getting engaged and having a ring like hers. Isn't it just fab., Emma? I wonder if I'll ever fall in love. I often think about it, don't you — what it'll feel like, I mean.'

Emma stayed silent. For the first time she and Lindy were apart in their experiences and Lindy seemed more than six months younger. Lindy was so uncomplicated — she just took life as it came and she never worried inside herself as Emma did. Once Mother had told her: 'You're far too sensitive, Emma. Don't take everything so seriously!' It was easy to say things like that but much harder to change yourself if that was the way you were made.

'Let's swim,' she said quickly before Lindy could repeat her question. 'I'll call the children!'

For a little while Emma was happy again. The four of them jostled and fooled around in the water and enjoyed the sunshine, the sea and the freedom. But when the younger children wandered away again to look for shells, she and Lindy lay once more on the sand sunbathing and her private thoughts flooded her mind again. She knew that she was really just waiting for Julie to arrive with Andrew.

Both families had come by car, crossing from Southampton to Cherbourg and driving down to the coast in easy stages. Andrew drove his family's Morris estate car most of the way, the children changing cars to vary the journey for themselves and their parents. Andrew was a good driver — fast but safe. Emma had loved the long hours sitting in the back seat with Penny and Paul, watching Andrew's long thin hands on the steering wheel; seeing the back of his head where the fair hair curled into his neck.

Andrew seemed to her to strike just the right balance between being modern without looking ridiculous as some boys did who grew their hair down to their shoulders. Emma couldn't stand the ones who looked like girls and yet she didn't like the old-fashioned cropped boy's cut either. It was the same with the clothes he wore — they were mod. without being extreme. Julie's, of course, were ultra modern. She liked immensely short skirts which showed off her long thin legs; and white toe-less boots and brilliant colours. She spent most of her secretarial pay on clothes and was always right up to date with the current fashion. Mother and Father had long since given up trying to sober Julie down and she chose her own clothes now she could pay for them herself. Julie had long straight fair hair which always hung over one side of her face and made Father tease her by lifting the soft fair curtain of hair so that he could 'see who he was talking to'. Julie didn't mind — she just laughed and told Father to 'get with it!'

'If only I could be like Julie!' Emma

thought. But her crisp dark hair had a natural wave and wouldn't lie flat, no matter what she did with it. If it was lacquered it just went sticky. Now already the sea air was making it curl in wisps and she knew she looked fourteen rather than nearly seventeen. But most of all she wished she had Julie's eyes, big slightly tilting eyes the colour of sapphires. She made the most of them, too, with lots of eye make-up that Mother objected to but which made her eyes seem twice as big again. Emma's eyes were the same shape but not so large and a dark brown so that she would never be able to accentuate their colour with eye shadow the way Julie could. Her skin, too, was different. It was olive rather than white like Julie's. Emma really only liked her skin in the summer when she turned a beautiful mahogany brown. Julie had to take care of her face or she burned badly and then her face would peel. As for poor Lindy — she just erupted into a positive crop of freckles and with her rather short, plump figure, looked anything but glamorous.

'We aren't either of us 'glamorous' types!' Emma thought with a sudden deep affection for her friend.

Her glance wandered across the sand to where the children were bent over their buckets of shells. Penny, her little sister, was obviously laying down the law to Paul who was looking at her, his head on one side. Emma could see Penny gesticulating with one hand as she waved the bucket with the other. How easy life had been at that age — nothing more important to worry about than who had found the shell first! She wished she were eight again. At that age, you didn't think about your face or your figure, about whether any boy would ever find you attractive enough to want to marry you; whether any boy could ever love you.

'I'm going to help them build a castle!' she told Lindy, jumping to her feet. 'Coming?'

They were soon deeply absorbed in

the task of building Mont St Michel in the sand when a voice caused Emma to look up from her labours.

'Mademoiselle?'

To her surprise, a strange young man in bathing trunks was addressing her.

'It's him — the French boy from the hotel!' Lindy whispered. Paul and Penny started to giggle and Emma blushed with sudden shyness.

'Shut up, you two!' she said violently.

'*Vous permettez?*' the French boy said, and to Emma's amazement, he went down on his knees and began to assist them with the sand castle. For a moment or two they all worked in silence. Then the French boy sat back on his heels and smiling, said:

'I cannot spik English very good but I try. This very fine castle — is Buckingham Palace, no?'

Penny shrieked with laughter.

'No, it's Mont St. Michel. We passed it on the road from Cherbourg.'

The boy smiled. Emma thought: 'He's shy like me!' Then he said:

'May I introduce me to you? My name is Yves Courtelle.'

Lindy took over the introductions, presenting Emma and the two children and herself. They all shook hands and resumed work on the castle. With great skill, Yves began to form the ramparts. The children stopped work to watch.

'You are clever!' Paul said admiringly.

'You must be an artist!' Lindy said.

'No, not artist. I study — how you say in English — the sculpture?'

'A sculptor!' Lindy cried. 'How exciting!'

Yves smiled and looked at Emma, who smiled back shyly.

'I have long to make beautiful sand castles but do not think big boy can do this alone. When I see you with children, I think this give me excuse to play in the sand like little child, yes?'

Penny and Paul burst out laughing again. Emma ssshed them violently, ashamed of them, but Yves did not seem in the least discomforted. He soon became absorbed once more in the castle.

When at last the finishing touches

had been made, they all sat back on their heels to admire it. Adults as well as children passing by stopped to admire the edifice. It really was a work of art. They were all flushed and pleased.

'How absolutely fab!'

Julie's voice startled all of them. She stood with Andrew looking down at them with her laughing eyes. Yves at once jumped to his feet and Emma hurriedly introduced him to Julie and Andrew. Yves bowed in continental fashion which sent the children into a fresh burst of laughter. Yves' face coloured, as if he were embarrassed suddenly at being caught at a child's game, but when Julie said again admiringly: 'It really is gorgeous!' he looked pleased and proud.

'Yves did most of it!' Lindy said. 'He's studying to be a sculptor. Isn't it exciting?'

Emma looked at Julie and caught the sudden glance of interest she gave the French boy. Andrew said abruptly:

'Come on, kids, it's time we were on our way back!'

But Julie shook her head.

'Don't let's go just yet, Andrew. The tide's coming in. We just must watch the waves come into the moat.'

She was wearing pale blue jeans and a white Tee-shirt. She was, as usual, looking lovely and quite unconscious of it. No wonder Yves couldn't take his eyes off her.

Andrew said sharply:

'Oh, do come along, Julie. It's half past five!'

'So what, darling,' Julie said pleasantly. 'There's no desperate hurry. Dinner isn't till eight, anyway. Besides, it's so lovely here on the beach. Do look at those French children. They're dying to get a closer look at the castle but they're too shy.' She turned to Yves in her usual easy manner. 'You tell them they can come and look if they want to!' she commanded him.

At once he did as she asked and the children gathered round, no longer shy, talking and admiring. Julie laughed.

'I thought I understood French but I certainly don't begin to understand them!' she said to Yves.

'They're talking the Breton dialect!' Yves explained. 'It is quite different from true French — how it is in England perhaps with the English and Welsh?'

He and Julie became involved in an animated conversation on Gaelic. Glancing at Andrew, Emma saw that he was glowering with annoyance. Was it because Julie had refused to break up the party? Or because he was jealous?

'Oh, poor Andrew!' she thought. Suddenly, she hated Julie for making him unhappy. Julie had no right . . . and yet she was obviously quite unconscious of Andrew's mood.

The younger children were helping Lindy to dig a trench from the sea to the castle moat. Everyone was absorbed in something except herself. And Andrew. If only she could think of something to say that would make him happy — as happy as Julie was. Desperately, she said:

'Julie's terribly thrilled about her ring, Andrew. It is a lovely one.'

Andrew looked down at her as if he had only just noticed her.

'I got it because it is just the colour of her eyes!' he said eagerly. 'Don't you agree, Emma?'

'Yes, I do. It's the perfect choice.'

Andrew looked at Julie with a strange uneasiness in his eyes.

'She's so lovely!' he said. 'Nothing is really good enough for her. I still find it difficult to believe we're really engaged. Sometimes I have to look down at that ring to make myself believe it's true! I wish she hadn't stopped wearing it.'

'Oh, but that's only because she's afraid of losing it!' Emma said quickly.

Andrew sighed.

'I know that's what she says but you don't just lose a ring, do you? I mean, it can't just drop off or anything.'

'But, Andrew, it's far too precious to wear all the time . . . ' Emma began, but broke off, knowing only too well that engagement rings were usually worn all the time. 'At least, not on a beach!'

Andrew suddenly put his arm round her shoulders.

'Dear little Emma!' he said warmly. 'You always did want to comfort everybody, didn't you? Even when you were very small you couldn't bear anyone to be hurt. I remember once, when you were little more than a toddler, I fell out of the apple tree and cut my leg pretty badly. You came rushing up and planted a big wet kiss on my good knee and said: That'll make it better!'

Emma felt the colour rushing into her cheeks. The touch of Andrew's arm across her shoulders, his words, affected her far more deeply than he could possibly realise. A compliment from him was worth more to her than . . . than any ring.

Andrew took his arm away and sighed.

'I suppose I'll have to learn to share Julie!' he said.

Julie's face was one of absorbed interest as she listened to what the French boy was saying. Every now and again she laughed, tossing her fair hair out of her eyes and throwing her head back. Knowing Julie as well as they both did, they knew that while not actually flirting, she was nevertheless aware of Yves' interest in her; was unconsciously playing up to it.

'I'm going back to wait by the car!' Andrew said, his face darkening. 'Perhaps you'll tell Julie where I am since she's obviously far too absorbed to notice my departure.'

He turned and walked quickly away. Emma followed him with her eyes, not knowing what she could do to help him. As he had said all too truly, Julie was not aware of his leaving.

'Julie!' Emma cried. 'Julie, it really *is* time we went home. It's nearly six!'

Julie turned a gay, happy face towards her sister.

'Oh, is it really?' she asked innocently. 'Well, we'd better make a move, I suppose. Are you coming, Yves? Can we give you a lift in the car?'

'Thank you very much,' the boy said. 'I like that very much as it is the long walk to the 'otel, no?'

'I just love listening to your accent!' Julie cried, her eyes sparkling. From anyone else, the remark might have seemed impertinent. But it was so obvious she really was fascinated that Yves, far from looking annoyed, looked very pleased indeed.

Andrew watched as they walked towards him, an untidy group carrying buckets and spades and bathing things. No one seemed to be talking now but he could see the French boy. He was holding Julie's arm.

3

That evening Yves was included in the family game of cards. One of the family favourites was Racing Demon, played with as many packs as there were players. The game was new to Yves and there was a good deal of teasing at the mistakes and confusion he caused amongst the more practised players. It was Julie who took him under her wing, stopping her own play to remind him to put on a Queen or put out an Ace.

Emma was surprised. Ever since Julie had been a tiny girl she had always wanted to win, whether it was a game of tennis, a swimming race or a simple game of cards. Not that she was a bad loser but whatever she undertook, it was always with the object of being first or best. That she readily put aside her own chances of winning by helping Yves was strange enough for Emma to notice: and, so it appeared, did Andrew.

Andrew became more and more silent and taciturn. Once or twice he spoke sharply to Julie telling her she was slowing up the game. Julie laughed.

'Well, it is only a game!' she said, shrugging her shoulders.

But gradually Emma sensed that it wasn't the game Andrew minded — it was Julie's obvious interest in Yves.

'He's jealous!' she thought as she and Lindy exchanged packs for shuffling. At once, her sympathies were with Andrew. Surely Julie could see that he was hurt by her attention to Yves. As Andrew's fiancée, she ought to think first of him. After all, she, Emma, or Lindy could assist Yves who was not quite as helpless as Julie was making out.

After the fourth game Andrew stood up and suggested to Julie a walk to the end of the jetty. Across the estuary lay the little town of Loctudy. A motor boat plied to and fro between there and the jetty and Andrew thought it might be fun to cross over and see what was doing on the other side.

Julie shook her head.

'I don't want to go tonight, Andrew!' she said. 'It's windy and I had more than enough wind sailing this afternoon. Let's have another game — or if you don't want to play Racing Demon, how about vingt-et-un? You must know that, Yves?'

The French boy nodded, smiling.

Andrew stood looking down at them all, his face flushed and angry. Emma felt her heart miss a beat. The palms of her hands were damp with nervousness. Didn't Julie understand that Andrew wanted her to himself? Or was she deliberately trying to annoy him? Make him even more jealous?

'I'm going anyway. If you don't want to come, Julie, I'll go on my own.'

Julie gave him a quick searching look. Now there was no doubting Andrew was upset, Emma thought. But Julie just said:

'I'd really rather not go tonight, Andrew. Tomorrow, perhaps!'

Emma, unable to take her eyes from Andrew's face, saw his expression of dismay.

'I'd like to go, Andrew. Could I go with you? And Lindy?'

Andrew barely glanced at her. He shrugged his shoulders and said:

'Okay, if you want! Better ask your mother first, though.'

Emma went off with Lindy to find their parents who were drinking coffee in the hotel bar. No one objected to the two girls going with Andrew, but when Emma returned to the lounge and saw Julie and Yves alone at the card table, she suddenly realised that her impulsive offer to go with Andrew so that he wouldn't have to be alone, had really only aggravated the situation. With her and Lindy and Andrew away, the little ones already in bed, it left Julie alone with Yves.

Andrew was uncommunicative as they stood on the jetty waiting for the ferry boat to reach them. They could see her lights approaching them across the water. Emma felt the wind tugging at her hair beneath her head scarf and tried to cover up Andrew's silence by chattering to Lindy. Lindy seemed quite unaware of the subterranean disquiet and announced well within Andrew's hearing that she thought Yves was going to make a good addition to their family party.

'He's here all alone with his parents who look terribly stuffy!' she said innocently. 'I expect it'll make the world of difference to his holiday to have some other young people to go around with. I just love the way he pronounces English words. Did you know he has his own boat here and sails a lot? Julie told me before dinner tonight that he has offered to take any of us sailing who wants to go.'

'And Mother had the good sense to forbid it!' Andrew broke in. 'Sailing can be dangerous if you don't know what you're doing. Besides, none of you can sail.'

'Except Julie!' Lindy interrupted

thoughtlessly. 'She can sail very well, Andrew — you said so yourself. You said you'd rather have her crew for you than any of your men friends.'

'That's different. Julie can be trusted with me. But none of us know if Yves Courtelle is any good with a boat, or how much he knows about local conditions.'

'Well, you know nothing about them!' Lindy said with sisterly honesty. Emma rushed to Andrew's defence.

'Andrew knows enough about sailing to go anywhere!'

Andrew shot her a surprised look. It was strange the way little Emma was always on his side. She was altogether a strange kid, he thought. Quiet, dreamy, usually the least noticeable member of their two families because she never asserted herself. Julie took most of the lime-light and the youngsters, Penny and Paul, grabbed what was left. Emma took such a long time to come out with anything that someone else had usually said it long before she spoke!

But he liked Emma. She was always kind and thoughtful of other people. No doubt her suggestion to come with him this evening had been as much for his sake as because she really wanted to go. But it had only made matters worse. Now Julie was alone with the French boy and Andrew didn't like it one bit.

It was strange, Andrew thought, that he'd never been particularly jealous until lately . . . until his engagement to Julie, in fact. In the past he'd accepted her constantly changing boy friends as a necessary part of her growing up; something that had to be endured whether he liked it or not. At least, none of them ever lasted very long and she always continued to see him throughout. He'd loved her even then, of course, but he had no real hope that Julie was in love with him. It wasn't until shortly before her twenty-first birthday that their friendship had suddenly taken a new turn. They'd been lying in the long grass near the tennis court in Andrew's garden. The younger children were out on a picnic somewhere. Julie was discussing the guests invited to her party.

'All your boy friends, I see!' Andrew had said.

Julie laughed.

'Ex-boy friends, you mean. You're my only permanent, Andy!'

He turned on his side and looked down at her for a long moment. Then he'd kissed her quickly but softly on her laughing mouth. The smile had faded from her eyes and she had a questioning look in them after that kiss.

'That's because I hope I'll go on being the only permanent. I love you very much, Julie. One day, I hope you'll fall in love with me, too.'

'You're teasing again, Andrew!' Julie had said, jumping to her feet and tossing her fair hair out of her eyes. But he knew that she didn't believe what she said. She merely had not wished to take his remark seriously.

Then the miracle happened at the

party. He wasn't quite sure what had made him buy the engagement ring except that he'd happened to notice it in the jeweller's shop when he was looking for a suitable birthday gift for her. Lindy had suggested a pendant and he'd set out to choose a pendant. Then his eye had been caught by the ring — by the brilliant sapphire blue stone and its exact resemblance to Julie's eyes. For a long moment of doubt he had hesitated. The jeweller, seeing his hesitation, had said:

'We are always prepared to buy back any of our goods. If your young lady doesn't care for the ring, we can easily change it.'

That was when he decided. If Julie refused it, he could take it back . . .

And she had not refused it. Even now, he could scarcely believe she was engaged to him, his fiancée. Even harder was it to believe that she loved him. For her behaviour had changed hardly at all since their engagement. She was still the casually affectionate girl he'd always known. Only when he kissed her goodnight was there any difference in Julie. Now her kisses, like his own, were no longer casual but increasingly passionate. Sex was rearing its ugly head in no uncertain fashion, Andrew told himself warningly, but could that be called love? On his side it most certainly was for he wanted her in every possible way; he loved everything about her and his physical need of her was no more than his need of her as a companion, a friend. He simply wasn't interested in any other girl, nor ever had been.

But Julie . . . somehow her reactions just weren't those of a girl madly in love. Her gay, friendly manner towards him, sometimes teasing, sometimes critical, hadn't been replaced with any new tenderness, closeness. She seemed in no hurry at all to fix a date, however distant, for their marriage.

'Not for ages and ages!' she'd said when he'd tried to pin her down. 'I'm just not ready to settle down and be a housewife yet, darling!'

That was really the whole trouble. Julie wasn't ready to settle down. The way she was behaving tonight with the French boy was little different from the pre-engagement Julie with a new boy friend. She seemed quite insensitive to Andrew's feelings about it. She didn't even want to be alone with him this evening. She preferred the company of another boy . . .

'Here's the boat, Andy!' His sister was tugging at his sleeve. Suddenly, Andrew made up his mind.

'I've decided not to go after all,' he said abruptly. 'Julie's right — it's far too windy. Sorry, girls.'

Lindy began to argue. She was disappointed, having made up her mind to enjoy this adventure. She thought it more than inconsiderate of her brother to let them down at the last minute. But Andrew was walking back towards the hotel, ignoring her complaints and it was left to Emma to explain to Lindy that Andy was upset about Yves.

Lindy linked her arm through Emma's and sighed.

'It's no use Andy getting into a tizz every time Julie looks at another boy. Julie's such a friendly type. New people interest her. He'll just lose her if he gets too possessive.'

Emma felt obliged to defend Andrew.

'He's very much in love with her,' she argued. 'And Julie's supposed to be in love with him. If I were her I'd have gone with Andrew this evening . . . '

Lindy squeezed her friend's arm.

'Oh, well, you're different, Emma. You always want to make everyone else happy all the time. Personally, I think Andrew was a fool to get engaged to your sister. He'd have done far better to wait for you.'

Emma felt the blood rushing to her cheeks. She thanked God for the darkness so that Lindy could not see her blushing.

'What nonsense!' she murmured, but Lindy wasn't listening.

'After all, you're seventeen next

birthday. Lots of girls of that age get engaged and even married. And you're much better suited to Andrew than Julie is. They're far too alike, I think. They're both got violent tempers and they both want to be best at everything, and look how they've quarrelled all through their childhood.'

'But never about anything important. They always made it up. I think they enjoy quarrelling.'

'Maybe!' Lindy agreed. 'But surely that's not what you want for a marriage. I'm not saying anything against Julie, Emma. I like her very much and I think she's frightfully pretty, too. But I just don't think she is right for Andrew!'

Emma was glad they had reached the hotel. Lindy's words were far more upsetting than she realised, confirming as they did Emma's own fears. And Lindy's views were less biased than her own might be since she had no personal axe to grind. Every nerve in her body cried out against Andrew's and Julie's engagement because she loved Andrew and would have given the rest of her life for him to be in love with her. She was ashamed of her feelings and yet she had to be honest with herself. She couldn't trust her own motives and because of that, she could never be Julie's confidant again. If Julie wanted to talk about Andrew it couldn't be to her, Emma. Whatever problems she might have, she must solve them herself. Not that Julie seemed to have any problems. She was as cheerful and uncomplicated as ever.

In the lounge Yves was sitting alone, playing a game of patience. In answer to Lindy's question he told them Andrew had taken Julie into the bar for some coffee.

'You stay to play another Demon Racing with me?' he asked with his shy smile.

Lindy shook her head, saying she was suddenly tired and would go to bed. Emma hesitated. She, too, was tired with the unaccustomed sea air and all the nervous tensions of the evening. But

Yves looked so lonely and she hesitated again.

'Do please stay!' he said.

So she sat down, calling to Lindy that she would be up in half an hour.

They played the game with serious concentration but when it was over — Emma having won despite her efforts not do so — Yves seemed inclined to talk. He wanted the two families separated.

'All is mixed at table and on the beach!' he said. 'I not know for sure who is sister and brother.'

Emma explained carefully. Yves looked puzzled.

'Your sister, Julie? She is not then sister also to Andrew?'

'No, certainly not!' Emma said, startled. 'They are engaged to be married. Fiancés.'

Yves looked astounded.

'This I did not know. Now I understand why Andrew look so angry with her when she would not go with him to Loctudy.' He looked at Emma in bewilderment. 'But why does she not go?'

Emma felt her cheeks burning.

'Probably she just didn't feel like it. She was right, too, it was very windy. That's why we came back.'

'She is to marry Andrew soon?'

She shook her head.

'Oh, no! They've only just got engaged — a few weeks ago actually. They won't get married for ages, I expect.'

Yves was silent, lost in thought for a moment. Emma took the opportunity to study him. He really was very handsome in a Continental way. He had beautiful large dark eyes that were very expressive. His face was a sensitive one and he seemed very intelligent. She wondered just how old he was, where he was studying sculpture. But before she could ask him, he clapped his hands together and cried out:

'Now I think I understand. This is the arranged marriage, is it not? Between the two families?'

'Oh, dear!' Emma felt herself blushing again. She knew from books she had read and from history about a mariage de convenance — arranged between two families for financial or other reasons or between aristocratic or royal families who for political reasons might find a family tie an advantage. 'In England we don't have this sort of arrangement any more,' she tried to explain. 'It used to happen in the olden days but never now.'

Yves subsided once more into thoughtfulness. But this time not for long. He looked at Emma with his attractive smile.

'This is not my affair, no? How do you say in English?'

'Not your business,' Emma translated literally, smiling in spite of herself.

'Business is work, is it not? You say in English that a man has his business in London, for example?'

They became involved in a discussion of colloquialisms. Emma was glad that, for the moment, they were off the subject of Julie and Andrew. Emma found that once Yves had lost his shyness, he was an easy and interesting conversationalist. He told her he was twenty-two, that he was a Parisien and had studied art, drawing, before he had decided to become a sculptor. But he was not sure he could make a living in this way and might have to revert to his drawing. His parents were quite well off but his pride forbade that he should continue to live indefinitely on the allowance they gave him. After the holiday, he was to begin a course in commercial art.

'I would like very much to do a portrait of Julie,' he said. 'I find her face quite fascinating. It is the formation of the bone. Do you think her fiancé would permit?'

'Andrew?' Emma tried to speak naturally. 'I don't suppose Andrew could stop Julie doing anything she wanted. Julie's very strong-willed.'

'Then it is incorrect for me to ask his permission?'

'I don't know. I . . . I don't think

Andrew would really mind but somehow I'm sure Julie would object if you
asked him and not her. I just don't
know, Yves.'

She certainly couldn't explain to him
that Andrew was already a little jealous
of him and that this would probably
add fuel to the flames. But since Yves
had really done nothing at all to
provoke Andrew's jealousy, it did seem
unreasonable. And Julie had only been
friendly and nice to Yves. There was no
just cause for Andrew's jealousy and
yet . . .

'Maybe I paint you instead?' Yves
said, smiling. 'You, too, have a very
interesting face. But with you it is more
the expression than the bones. You
and your sister are not at all alike — the
opposite of each other, no?'

Emma, embarrassed as always by
anything personal, stood up and held
out her hand.

'I really must go up to bed. Lindy
will be waiting . . . ' she said hurriedly.
'Thank you for the game.'

If Yves was surprised at her abrupt departure, he did not show it. He sat down after she had left and dealt out another hand of patience. But he played automatically, his thoughts caught up with the two girls — the elder so pretty and friendly and gay; the younger so serious, so intense with those dark thoughtful eyes. He had thought that on this holiday he had agreed to to please his parents, he would have only his sailing to entertain him. Now he knew that there was to be a good deal more. People were an endless fascination for him. To be a good artist, he knew that he must study human beings, see beneath the surface they showed to the world. And not the least interesting thing he had discovered so far was the curious relationship between the English man Andrew, and Julie. And of one thing he was already certain — she was not the least in love with him. Why, then, should she agree to marry him? It was a question the younger sister had not so far managed to explain.

4

'Of course I'm not going to stop talking to Yves!' Julie's eyes were sparkling with anger. 'Why on earth should I?'

'If for no other reason, then because I ask you!' Andrew retorted scowling.

They were walking along the beach without any particular destination in mind. It was too windy for sailing which was a disappointment to them both and Andrew, who had wanted to visit Loctudy the previous evening, perversely refused to go this morning. To Julie, he seemed to be in a thoroughly truculent mood but to please him she had agreed to the walk along the sands rather than do as she would have liked and join the family party going across in the ferry.

Now, instead of being particularly grateful and pleased to have her to himself, Andrew had accused her of flirting with the French boy. Julie felt she was justifiably angry.

'But why should you ask me anything so stupid?' she flashed back at him. With her bare toes, she was scuffling up the dry sand as she walked. The wind was blowing it away at once in the direction of the sea which looked grey, turbulent and angry. Loose sand was also blowing off the dunes against their legs and faces, stinging and unpleasant.

'I don't know what's got into you, Julie!' Andrew said accusingly. 'You're just trying to make me angry. You want a quarrel!'

'I never heard anything more silly. You're the one who has been trying to quarrel ever since we came out here. Look at the way you behaved last night. First you wanted to go to Loctudy and then you didn't, so I stopped my game of cards and went to have a drink with you. Then, instead of being grateful, you were surly and refused to say two words to me. And now this — this stupid nonsense about Yves Courtelle.'

Andrew's mouth tightened.

'I take it from your last remark that you would have preferred to continue your game with Courtelle rather than have a drink with me?'

Julie stopped walking and stamped her foot in the sand.

'You're being quite ridiculous, Andrew. I didn't say that. I said that the way you behaved when I *did* go with you made me wonder if I wouldn't have had more fun staying with Yves. And that goes for this morning, too. I bet the rest of the family aren't arguing about nothing.'

'I thought you were very anxious to go to Loctudy with them. Now I understand — Yves went with them.'

They stood facing each other, frowning and furious.

'I'm going back to the hotel. You just don't know how silly you're being, Andrew. I like Yves — we all like him, except you, it seems. But I have *not* been flirting with him and I did not want to go to Loctudy this morning because he was going. So believe it or not as you wish.'

She turned and began to march back the way they had come.

Andrew hurried after her, catching hold of her arm. But she twisted free. He caught up with her a second time and said:

'You seem to be forgetting that you're engaged to me now, Julie. What kind of a fool do you think it makes me look when you are clearly fascinated by another man?'

Julie's space slowed and her face softened a little.

'You really are being an idiot, Andy. You're jealous for absolutely no reason at all. I've told you I just like him — that's all. You're imagining the rest. As to me making you look a fool, I think you're the one who's making a fool of yourself.'

Andrew's voice was also mollified. He said:

'Well, I'm sorry if I have annoyed you but I don't think you realise when you are flirting and when you aren't.

Maybe I am jealous . . . I suppose I am. But it's only because I love you so very much, darling.'

Julie stopped and turned impulsively to plant a kiss on his cheek.

'Silly old Andy. All the same, we'd better get this thrashed out once and for all.' Her blue eyes darkened thoughtfully. 'The fact is I like people — all people. They interest me and sometimes, I suppose, I interest them. I can't suddenly exclude all unmarried males just because you're going to blow your top thinking I'm falling in love or something crazy like that. It's positively Victorian behaviour, Andy.'

Andy grinned disarmingly.

'I suppose you're right. All the same, darling, I do wish you'd wear your ring. Then Yves and all the rest to come would know right off you were my girl.'

Julie pouted.

'Well, you know the reason I don't wear it out here. I love that ring, Andy, and I'd hate to lose it. But if it'll stop all this nonsense, then I'll wear it provided you take full responsibility. Not that you could replace it if I lost it — you said it was an antique ring and unique.'

'Yes, I know, Julie, and it's true and you're perfectly right, of course. It is risky. But I would like you to wear it.'

'Then I will, you silly old darling. Don't you think I want to wear it? It's the most beautiful thing I've ever owned.'

Andrew linked his arm in hers and they retraced their steps walking slowly now, their paces matched. He was feeling happier and not a little ashamed of himself for the fuss he'd been making about Yves. But a little of the hurt still remained. If Julie was really as much in love with him as he was with her, she ought not to be in the very least bit interested in any other man. *He* hadn't even noticed if there was another girl in the hotel so why should she have noticed Yves! But he knew that wasn't quite fair — Yves had been the one to notice Julie and to find the family down on the beach yesterday. It had been clever of him to get to know the younger ones first — provide himself with an introduction to Julie . . .

He caught himself up quickly. Jealousy was a horrible trait and Julie was right to despise him for it. Besides, he should trust her as she trusted him. She loved him; she'd agreed to marry him one day and she had accepted his ring . . .

Again an unpleasant thought struck him. That ring — Julie said it was the most beautiful thing she'd ever owned. Could she have been influenced by her admiration for it; was that one of the factors that had decided her acceptance of his proposal?

'Now you really are getting silly!' he chided himself. He simply did not understand what had got into him all of a sudden. He'd never been suspicious and mistrustful of people before. In all the years he'd known Julie, his relationship with her had been devoid of any such morbid soul-searchings and doubts. It was only since their engagement — and that was the silliest part of it. He ought to be more and not less sure of her now they were engaged. Maybe he was just finding it difficult to believe she had suddenly fallen in love with him — after years of meaning no more to her than the-boy-next-door; a sort of brother and friend, but never a sweetheart. He'd all but despaired she would ever wake up one day to the discovery that she loved him so it wasn't surprising he was finding it hard to realise the miracle had finally happened.

Andrew sighed. The sound was lost in the noise of the wind. He wondered if it was the change in the weather that was causing his depression. Yesterday, their first full day here, had been so sunny and warm, everything sparkling in the sunshine. He and Julie had had a wonderful day sailing. She had looked so fabulous in tight white slacks and black polo-neck shirt. But then Julie always did look marvellous. Even in the old blue jeans she wore now which he'd see a hundred times at home, she still looked 'special' in some way.

'I love you so much, Julie!' he spoke his thoughts aloud. 'I don't know what I'd do if I lost you now.'

Julie laughed uneasily. What was wrong with Andrew? He was beginning to make her feel depressed. Yes, and doubtful. If he was going to be like this all the holiday, it would have a serious effect on her. She liked everything to be happy and gay and amusing. She had no time for self-analysis and probings into her emotions. Emma was the one who did all the deep thinking! Dear Emma — such a serious kid and in Julie's eyes, far too sensitive. If you were like Emma, you were bound to get hurt sooner or later. Emma minded too much about everything. She hoped so much that when Emma did have a boy friend, it would be someone like Andrew who was always kind. Andrew couldn't hurt anyone deliberately. He, like Emma, was far too easily hurt. They were really rather alike.

'Emma adores you,' Julie also spoke

her thoughts aloud. 'She always takes your side, Andrew. Do you know, she told me off this morning for being horrid to you. She said you were upset because of Yves and I didn't believe her. But she was right.'

'Emma's much more far-seeing than people are apt to realise!' Andrew said. 'Just because she doesn't say much, it doesn't mean she isn't thinking and feeling just as deeply as other people — maybe more so. I've a lot of time for Emma. She's very sweet.'

Julie laughed, her eyes sparkling again but this time teasingly.

'Now whose turn is it to be jealous? Any more praise of my little sister and I'll begin to think you'd rather be engaged to her than to me!'

'Julie . . . ' Andrew began but broke off, realising Julie was not serious. He, too, laughed. 'Perhaps if you don't behave yourself, I'll change my mind and take Emma instead. After all, she's almost seventeen. I forget sometimes how grown-up she is. Almost a woman.'

'Maybe she and Yves will fall madly in love and then neither of us need be jealous!'

There were few people on the beach — the French unlike the English, unwilling to submit to the blowing sand and cold wind. With a quick look around, Andrew caught Julie in his arms and gave her a long kiss. She responded warmly, rubbing her cheek against his and kissing the cold tip of his nose.

Andrew pulled her closer but now she was not so responsive. She seemed half afraid of the passion that she was only newly discovering in him. Most of the time he had himself under a tight control, knowing that with a very long engagement ahead, they must not let their emotions get out of hand. He respected Julie and her family and somehow couldn't contemplate behaving with Julie as he might have done with some other girl. He wanted to keep her as she was, completely innocent, until their wedding day. There would be no anticipating that day if he could help it. But despite this resolve, sometimes his need for her was so sudden and so strong that he was unable to hide it. On this, the third occasion he'd revealed his desire for her, Julie reacted in the same way as on the other occasions — she twisted out of his arms, nervous and unsure of herself.

Andrew wanted desperately to believe that this was a normal and expected reaction from anyone as young and innocent as Julie. But somehow, he was still hurt by it. He understood that what she did was right and yet he questioned whether a girl deeply in love would be able to tear herself away so easily; in fact so anxiously. Perhaps she did not feel she could trust him. Yet she must know he would never hurt her in any way; never allow himself to lose complete control.

Maybe when they were more used to being engaged, they would be able to talk about this. At present, they spoke of jobs and homes and marriage in general terms but without reference to sex. Andrew felt it was important to both of them that they should feel free to discuss everything. Maybe now was the time to question her; find out what her feelings really were. But he remained silent. Why, he was not sure but he suspected that it was fear; fear that Julie in her bright, thoughtless way, might say: 'Oh, Andrew, I just don't feel that way about you!' And if she were to say such a thing, he wasn't sure if he could bear the hurt that would result.

They were once more walking in silence, each lost in their own thoughts. Julie guessed that Andrew had been puzzled because she'd backed out of that embrace. In a way her own behaviour puzzled her. She wasn't as innocent as Andrew imagined, for there had been several occasions when she'd become momentarily rather keen on one of her boy friends and they'd indulged in some prolonged smooching sessions. She knew very well that her emotions were perfectly normal and healthy and once or twice when she had stopped to consider it, she'd been surprised at herself for remaining a virgin when so many of her friends were not. She could think of other men as lovers; she could think of Andrew as her husband but somehow she could not think of Andrew as her lover. She knew this did not make sense, especially as she found Andrew very attractive and loved it when he kissed her, held her hand, held her in his arms. But beyond that she felt a kind of barrier between them. Of course, she told herself, this would wear off when she became used to the idea of being engaged to him. It would have to wear off because she certainly couldn't go on refusing to behave as any other fiancée would behave. Several of her girl friends considered when they were engaged that it was perfectly all right to go the whole way. And Andrew wasn't asking that . . .

'Oh, dear!' Julie thought. 'I'm almost

wishing I wasn't engaged. It's making life so complicated!'

As if to confirm her feelings, Andrew said suddenly:

'Let's go over to Loctudy after all. It's only a small place so we're sure to run into the others.'

Suddenly, Julie wanted exactly the same thing, however little she understood Andrew's extraordinary *volte face*. She wanted the simple uncomplicated company of her younger sister and brother; of her parents and Andrew's family.

'All right, let's run!' she said eagerly. 'Look, Andrew, there's the ferry coming over from Loctudy now. If we hurry, we might just catch it before it goes back again.'

They raced across the sand, Andrew keeping pace with Julie's shorter stride. Presently they arrived breathless, at the jetty and were just in time to fling themselves into the boat before it set off again.

It was less than a five minute trip

across the water and they needed this time to get back their breath. Andrew sat with his arm round Julie's shoulder, his body protecting her from the full rush of the wind in her face.

'He is a darling!' she thought, then she forgot Andrew, for there on the approaching jetty stood someone she thought she recognised and yet who was still a little too far off for her to be sure.

'Look, Andrew,' she said pointing eagerly. 'Isn't that . . . '

'Yes!' Andrew interrupted coldly, withdrawing his arm. 'That's Yves!'

5

Yves reached down to help Julie out of the motorboat. His welcoming smile, however, included them both.

'Your families are just coming!' he told them. 'There is very little to see or do and they have decided to return to the hotel. I think perhaps it is necessary to go to Benodet for the shopping.'

'Isn't it worth a look round?' Julie asked.

Yves shrugged his shoulders.

'Really there is nothing much to see!'

Andrew stood silent and uncertain. Everything seemed to be going wrong with any plan he made. Now he'd brought Julie over here to find everyone else about to return. It really was annoying. He glanced up the street which led on to the jetty and could see nothing attractive or interesting. They would just have to go back in the ferry with the others.

At that moment their families came out of a shop and came walking towards them in small groups. The younger children ran ahead, recognising them and waving.

'We've bought some postcards for Granny and Grandpa!' little Penny shouted as soon as she was close enough. 'Look, Julie! Look, Andrew — the picture is of a real Breton fisherman.'

'We've got some French stamps, too!' Paul also showed his postcard. Emma joined them, confirming Yves' comment that there was little point in walking round Loctudy. She glanced up at Andrew and saw his scowl; wondered if he had had yet another quarrel with Julie. Her sister, however, seemed in the best of spirits and was chattering animatedly to Yves. Emma gave an inward sigh. Julie was so tactless sometimes. She didn't seem to have the least idea that Andrew was watching her and not enjoying seeing her get along so well with the French boy.

As their parents approached and the conversation became general, Emma stood a little apart from the group, lost in thought. In Julie's absence, Yves had devoted himself to her, Emma. And whilst she was not for one moment any the less in love with Andrew, she had enjoyed having a good-looking and charming boy escorting her; talking to her not as if she were a schoolgirl but as a grown woman. Now Julie had re-appropriated him without the least idea of Emma's or Andrew's feelings. That was the trouble with Julie — she never stopped to think what she was doing — she just acted instinctively. She was behaving as if she was about to fall in love with Yves. Of course, the thought was absurd. They'd only just met and anyway, Julie was engaged to Andrew. Yet improbable though the idea was, it could happen and at once her imagination saw Andrew's subsequent hurt and herself, Emma, there to console him.

'Really, Emma!' she told herself

disgustedly. 'You think like some stupid novelette. Julie loves Andrew and even if she didn't, Andrew wouldn't look twice at you. Next thing, you'll be *hoping* it will happen and that's a horrible thought to have. Besides, if I really love Andrew the way I think I do, I'd want him to be happy — not heart broken just so that I . . . '

'Emma!' Lindy's voice jolted her out of her daydream. 'Do hurry up — we'll miss the ferry!'

The rest of the party were already in the boat. It was quite a squash when Lindy and Emma clambered in with the others. Julie sat opposite Emma, between Andrew and Yves. In spite of the noise of the engine and the wind, she was endeavouring to carry on a conversation with both of them.

She looked so lovely, Emma thought, and quite unconscious of the picture she made with her long fair hair blowing across her face, her eyes sparkling with amusement at some joke Yves had made; her long slender legs in their tight jeans stretched out with natural grace in front of her. Emma was suddenly conscious of the contrast she herself must make. Whenever she wore jeans, they seemed to make her look like a boy, not like a girl in boy's clothing which was quite different. She was too thin — too angular, and her short curly hair didn't help towards a glamorous image either.

Suddenly Yves leant forward and said:

'You're not cold, are you? You take my coat?'

He was sufficiently observant to notice her shiver. It was not really cold and she wore a thick green jersey over her grey jeans. She was grateful to him for noticing. He *was* nice . . . Maybe if she didn't love Andrew so much she would have fallen a little in love with Yves. Lindy had already announced privately to Emma that she had a 'pash' on Yves. But then Lindy, this holidays, seemed to belong more with the younger children; to be still a schoolgirl thinking in schoolgirl jargon. Lindy didn't know what it was to be really in love. It made it impossible for her to confide in Lindy any more. There wasn't a living soul whom she could tell how she felt about Andrew. The secret had to be locked forever in her diary. She *could* tell Mother but she had no wish to do so. Mother was understanding and always did her best to help when anything went wrong, but she, too, still thought of Emma as a schoolgirl. She might relegate Emma's feelings for Andrew to the same level as Lindy's for Yves and Emma couldn't have borne that. Nor was it true. What she felt for Andrew was real love — the kind of love that endured everything; was willing to sacrifice everything. She'd go to the ends of the world for Andrew. So far there had been no opportunity to prove her love in any way. But although she knew there could be no reward, she was still ready and anxious to do something positive for him.

At lunch, the afternoon's entertainment came under discussion. Yves suggested they go sailing. Andrew said it was still too windy and Yves replied, that in his view conditions were not dangerous in any way. Andrew, stiff-lipped, insisted they were.

Julie wanted to go.

'Oh, do let's, Andrew!' she cried persuasively. 'It'll be fun. You know there wasn't really *enough* wind yesterday and with three of us crewing it shouldn't be difficult. Do let's go, darling!'

'I'm sorry, but I just can't agree, Julie!' Andrew said firmly. 'I'm not going and I don't want you to go either.'

Emma saw the sudden rush of colour flare into Julie's cheeks. She knew her sister's obstinacy. One had only to 'dare' Julie to anything to make her do it instantly; to forbid something to make it even more desirable. Before Julie could say anything, Emma broke in:

'I think Andrew's right, Julie. Father would never allow it on a day like this.'

Julie looked at her younger sister scornfully.

'What on earth has Father got to do with it? He's never sailed in his life and he can't possibly judge whether it's safe or not. If Yves says he's going, then I'm going, too. Andrew's just making difficulties for his own reasons!'

She might as well have said 'Andrew's jealous'. They all knew what she meant. Yves looked away embarrassed. Andrew's face tightened with anger.

'Go if you want then,' he said furiously to Julie, and to Emma's dismay, he got up and left the table.

The families had rearranged their seating places, leaving the grown-ups at one table, Yves joining the young ones at their table. Now Andrew's mother leant over and said anxiously:

'Isn't Andrew feeling well?'

'No, he's not!' Emma said swiftly, knowing the real reason for Andrew's departure could never be explained in the middle of the dining room. Anyway, it was better to leave the grown-ups out of it.

'Oh, *bother* Andrew!' Julie said softly. 'Why does he want to *spoil* everything!'

Emma rushed once more to his defence.

'You know that isn't fair, Julie. He's just anxious about your safety and that's understandable enough since you're his fiancée.'

Julie gave her sister an angry glance.

'Then maybe I made a mistake getting engaged!' she flashed back at Emma. 'I'm not a helpless little fool who needs looking after as if I were — Penny's age.'

Penny looked up indignantly.

'I'm not a silly little fool!' she said.

'Why's Andrew gone?' Paul asked curiously.

Fortunately the waitress with the meat course put an end to the children's questions. When she had finished serving them, Julie turned to Emma.

'Honestly, Em, Andrew's behaving like a . . . well, in a way I'm finding very tiresome.'

'You don't still mean to go, do you?' Emma asked anxiously.

'Yes, of course I do!' Julie retorted. 'Why shouldn't I go if I want?'

'Maybe it was a silly idea to suggest!' Yves interposed awkwardly. 'I think perhaps it is best we do not go, Julie.'

Emma let out her breath. It was nice of Yves to be so tactful. But Julie would have none of it.

'I shall go on my own then,' she said challengingly to Yves.

He looked at her uncertainly.

'But that really would not be safe. We can go another time . . . '

'We can go this afternoon!' Julie interrupted. 'Don't tell me you're afraid now, Yves?'

He shrugged his shoulders in a typically French manner.

'In my view there is no danger so I am not afraid. But I do not wish to be the cause of trouble between you and your fiancé. I think it best we don't go.'

Julie put down her knife and fork and her pretty mouth was hardening into a stubborn line Emma recognised.

'I *want* to go,' she said, 'and Andrew is not — I repeat not — going to be allowed to stop me.'

After lunch Yves managed to draw Emma apart from the others.

'I do not know what is best to do,' he said. 'If I do not agree to go, do you think your sister will go on her own?'

Emma sighed.

'I suppose she might. She's capable of it although she'd certainly not be able to handle a boat on her own in calm weather let alone in this wind.'

'Is it possible you could talk to her fiancé? Explain this to him and ask him please to come, too, if he so wishes.'

'I'm afraid he won't,' Emma said. 'Andrew's as stubborn as Julie. I'll try, though.'

She went upstairs and knocked on Andrew's door. He called to her to come in but his face fell when he saw her. He had obviously been hoping it would be Julie.

Emma haltingly explained that Yves wished him to go with Julie and him.

'Honestly, Andrew, Yves wants you to go, too. Yves is really very nice and I'm sure he doesn't mean to come between you and Julie in any way.'

'You don't know what you're talking about, Emma!' Andrew said roughly. He turned away and walked over to the window where he stood looking out over the grey turbulent water on which the anchored boats were bobbing playfully. 'Of course he finds her attractive and no doubt he thinks all is fair in love and war.'

'But, Andrew, he's no different with Julie than he was with me this morning when Julie wasn't there. He's just naturally attentive and charming.'

Andrew's voice was bitter.

'And no doubt Julie finds him as attentive and charming as you do, Emma, and much more of a novelty than I am. I'm beginning to think

Julie's no more in love with me than . . . well, than you are!'

He was quite unprepared for the violent rush of colour to Emma's cheeks although she quickly covered her face with her hands. Although he didn't realise what he had done, he was aware that he had embarrassed her. He suddenly wondered if little Emma thought herself in love with him. She had always hero-worshipped him and no one took it seriously. She was still just a kid.

'Emma!' he said gently. He went across the room and touched her arm affectionately. 'You are a silly little goose. If you want a hero to worship, you've picked quite the wrong person in me. I'm no hero; I'm very ordinary and I'm beginning to believe a very dull young man of twenty-two who has made an utter fool of himself.'

'You're not dull — and you're not ordinary!' Emma cried, no longer caring any more what she revealed. She couldn't bear Andrew to be in this self-deprecating mood. 'I think Julie is the luckiest girl in the world being engaged to you and as to her liking Yves better than you — why, that's just ridiculous. She doesn't even know him.'

'But she's not wasting any time getting to know him, is she?' Andrew commented bitterly, forgetting Emma again.

Emma was silent. Even if Julie wasn't encouraging Yves, she certainly wasn't discouraging him. At last she found something to say which might cheer Andrew up.

'Yves didn't know until last night that you and Julie were engaged. He was asking me about you both and he seemed surprised when I told him. I'm sure he isn't trying to take Julie away from you, Andrew. You're just imagining things. And you know Julie as well as I do — the more against Yves you seem to be, the more determined she'll be to stand up for him.'

Andrew sighed.

'Yes, that's true enough. But I simply

don't understand why she should if she really loves me. I honestly don't think she *is* in love with me, Emma. That's the awful part about all this. I know jealousy is an ugly thing and Julie hates it when I'm being possessive but I don't seem able to help myself. I suppose I just don't trust her — that's the difficulty. If I did, I wouldn't mind whom she talked to and smiled at.'

Loyally, Emma tried to defend her sister.

'She doesn't mean to hurt you, Andrew. She's just — well, just Julie. She doesn't stop to think — she rushes into things on the spur of the moment. I'm sure she'd never hurt you deliberately.'

Andrew looked down at Emma with real affection.

'That's one of the qualities I most admire in you, Emma. You're always loyal. One day some chap's going to count himself very lucky to have you for his girl. I'm sure you aren't capable of hurting anyone, even accidentally.'

Emma blushed.

'That isn't true, Andrew. I'm not really a very nice person. It's just that my faults don't show!'

Andrew laughed disbelievingly.

'And what faults have you been concealing from us all these years?'

'Well, I'm jealous, too, and envious of other people . . . ' Emma said haltingly. She couldn't say 'of Julie'. She didn't mind Andrew knowing she was very fond of him but he must never know she loved him . . .

Andrew seemed to have forgotten her. He was staring out of the window again, his face brooding.

'I suppose Julie's determined to go sailing, whatever I say. But I'm not going back on my word now. I shan't go with them. Let Julie have her afternoon with Yves. Maybe it's the best thing. If she is going to fall in love with him, the sooner I know it the better.'

Emma bit her lip.

'Are you sure that's wise, Andrew — sort of throwing them together?

Surely you could go, too? Julie wants you to, I know she does. And Yves asked me to ask you to join them. He's thoroughly embarrassed by the whole thing.'

'Let him be!' Andrew replied. 'I can't see why we have to have him tagging along with us anyhow. He's nothing to do with our party. Just my luck he had to come to this hotel the same fortnight we're here.' He turned back to Emma and his face softened. 'Now I suppose I'm being selfish. It's more fun for you and Lindy to have a young man around. If only Julie . . . ' he broke off, his face miserable.

Emma longed to go to him, put her arms round him and tell him to stop being unhappy; that even if Julie didn't love him, *she* did. But she knew that would be no consolation to Andrew. It was Julie he loved. She, Emma, meant no more to him than a little sister.

Andrew said:

'Well, if they're going off, that leaves the rest of us at a loose end. I'll drive you younger ones into St. Marine, if you like. There's a car ferry crosses to Benodet which will amuse the kids. Be something to do. The beach will be too windy for swimming.'

Emma turned to go. At the door she hesitated.

'Will you tell Julie?'

Andrew frowned.

'No, you can tell her — if she's interested, which I doubt. If I speak to her we shall only have another argument. It seems we can't talk to each other now without arguing.'

As she went downstairs, Emma thought how true Andrew's last words were. Somehow she must try to think up a way to break the present pattern. The more Andrew resented Julie's friendship with Yves, the more Julie resented him. The holiday would be completely spoilt if they went on like this. She couldn't bear to see Andrew so unhappy. Somehow she must bring herself to talk to Julie; find out if she really was interested in the French boy or only enjoying a mild flirtation to annoy Andrew. Perhaps she could make Julie see how miserable Andrew was.

But when she entered the lounge, it was to see Julie and Yves laughing together as if neither were the least bit concerned about anyone else.

'Julie!' Emma interrupted them, her voice sharper than she had intended. 'Andrew asked me to tell you he wouldn't be going with you this afternoon. He's taking Lindy and me and the younger ones to see the car ferry.'

Julie pushed the fair hair out of her eyes and looked at her younger sister with a shrug of her shoulders.

'That's okay by me. If he wants to be a spoil-sport, then let him. I'm getting a bit fed up with Andrew. He just wants to stop me having fun.'

'That's not true!' Emma said hotly, hating Julie in that moment for saying such things about Andrew in front of Yves, a stranger.

'That's right — you defend him!'

Julie flashed back. 'Just because you think Andrew is perfect, it doesn't make me blind to his faults. Go and enjoy his company with my blessing, Emma, and I just hope he's a little less bad tempered with you than he is with me. Come on, Yves.'

Yves hesitated, looking from Emma to Julie uneasily. But Julie was giving him no opportunity to back out of the arrangement.

'We're wasting time,' she said impatiently. 'I'll go and get my things and meet you on the jetty in five minutes. Okay?'

Yves, with the slightest shrug of his shoulders, nodded politely to Emma and went upstairs to change his clothes.

'You're not considering Andrew at all!' Emma said to Julie. 'He's frightfully upset!'

'That's his fault, not mine!' Julie said quickly, and with a toss of her head, she left Emma standing alone and deeply worried, staring after her.

6

Andrew was right — the water was rougher than Yves had supposed and good sailor though he was, he felt uneasy with only Julie for crew. It was already clear to him that she was relatively inexperienced and he decided to let the wind and current take them up the estuary to Benodet.

There was far too much for him to do to be able to talk to Julie other than to give her necessary instructions. She obeyed at once and seemed totally unaware of the trickiness of the sailing conditions. Or if she was, she appeared quite fearless. Yves was impressed. A French girl in similar circumstances might well become panicky. Julie was calm and seemed to be enjoying herself despite the fact that in a very short while, both of them were soaking wet.

But even as he worked busily at the boat, Yves had time to think. The fact was, Julie Prescott fascinated him. She was quite different from any of the girls he'd known at art school; different, too, from the well brought up young girls his parents occasionally presented to him in the hope that he would eventually marry one of them. They were always anxious lest he should become involved with an 'unsuitable' girl! They knew nothing, of course, of the various love affairs he'd had from time to time. That side of his life would not concern them until marriage came into the picture and so far, he'd not met any girl he wanted to be married to for the rest of his life.

Yves had firm ideas about his future wife. For one thing, he would not marry for money — indeed, for anything but love. He was an idealist and he wanted the perfect companion when he married. The eligible daughters of his parents' friends did not interest him with or without dowries. If he fell in love, he'd marry with or without money.

Julie Prescott he found exciting and attractive. He was also intrigued by the curious relationship that seemed to exist between her and her fiancé. It simply did not make sense to him. The younger sister, Emma, had told him this was not a marriage of convenience; therefore it had to be supposed they were in love with each other. Yet while Andrew manifested all the obvious signs of being in love with Julie, the girl seemed anything but in love with Andrew. If anything, it was the younger girl who appeared to be in love with Andrew.

Emma, also, interested Yves. Her quietness, which at first might be mistaken for dullness, was really only the cover for a deeply emotional young woman. And though her family might treat her as a young schoolgirl, it was clear to Yves that she was far more mature than the other young girl, Lindy; indeed, in some ways more mature than her elder sister! One day she would be far more beautiful than Julie. At present, her small pointed face had a coltish angularity that did not do justice to the beautiful bone structure. When she filled out a little she would be really lovely. Her smile did not appear often, but when it did, it transformed her face, filling it with warmth and light. He would like to paint both girls — so different despite their identical parentage.

Yves had to use all his concentration to get the little boat beached. When at last the job was done, he was soaked to the skin. Julie was standing on the beach, laughing at him.

'You look like a drowned rat!' she said. 'And I suppose I do, too. Let's go and get some hot coffee. There must be a café somewhere near. Maybe we'll run into the others and we can get a lift back in the car.'

Yves glanced round and saw that they were only a few hundred yards from the little town where they could surely find several cafés in which to have a hot drink. If they did not run into the rest of the party, they could cross to St. Marine in the ferry and hitch a lift back to Île Tudy. Julie was quite right — a drink would warm them up a little. The wind against their wet clothes was chilling.

They hurried into the town and soon discovered a pâtisserie where they ordered hot chocolate and Julie a huge chocolate éclair. It amused Yves to see her tucking into it with no regard for her figure. But then she was slender enough. Like Emma, she could afford to put on weight.

Presently, when she had finished eating, Julie turned to him with a satisfied smile.

'It has been fun!' she said. 'I suppose Andrew will say 'I told you so!' when he hears we had to beach the boat, but that won't bother me. I've enjoyed it enormously.'

'So have I!' said Yves. 'All the same, your fiancé was quite right — it was really too rough to be safe. We were once or twice lucky not to . . . how do you say in English, turn over in the water?'

'Capsize!' Julie told him. 'Well, even if we had, we could have swum to the beach. We were never very far off shore except round the rocks.'

'That was the dangerous part!' Yves told her. 'The current there is very strong. One or two times I was afraid.'

'Well, I wasn't. I thought you managed the boat wonderfully!' Julie laughed happily, enjoying the thought of danger in retrospect. 'I think Andrew was silly not to come, too.'

'I think he is very angry that you come with me,' Yves said. 'And for this one cannot blame him. In his place I, too, would be angry.'

Julie looked at Yves with raised eyebrows.

'I don't see why. I'm not married to Andrew, even if I am engaged. And anyway, I don't see what right he has to do me out of an afternoon's fun. He's just jealous, that's all.'

'Is that not enough? I, too, would be jealous if my fiancée preferred the company of another man.'

Julie grinned mischievously.

'Oh, well, I suppose so. But it's all so silly. I'm not going to stop talking to any other man just because I'm engaged. That's old-fashioned and silly.'

Yves gave the slightest shrug of his shoulders.

'Love is not, how do you say? — a question of fashion. If one is in love, then one wishes to keep the beloved to oneself, no?'

Julie laughed.

'I just adore your English!' she said. 'But I know what you mean. I suppose you're right but I can't seem to be that way with Andrew. After all, I've known him almost all my life and it would be silly for the two of us to go around wrapped up in each other, to the exclusion of everyone else. I don't feel that way about Andrew.'

'But this is the way he feels about you!' Yves said dryly.

Julie sighed.

'I suppose so. Maybe I'm just not in love that way. I adore Andrew and one day I'll be married to him and we'll have lots of fun together. But he'll have to stop being jealous.'

'And you will have to stop making him jealous.'

Julie's eyes twinkled with mischief.

'Honestly, Yves, I didn't do it on purpose. You suggested we all go sailing and I agreed it would be fun. That's all there was to it.'

'If I were engaged to a girl as pretty as you, Julie, I, too, would be afraid of other men finding her attractive.'

Julie looked at her companion, her mouth twitching. Her eyes were full of laughter.

'You think I am attractive, then?' she asked.

'I do most certainly. And I think your Andrew knows it, and he doesn't like it.'

'But I like it,' Julie said pouting. 'And I don't see why I shouldn't have any fun just because I'm engaged. I'm only twenty-one and I don't want to get married for ages and ages yet.'

Yves gave his now familiar little shrug of incomprehension.

'If you love him very much, surely you wish very soon to be married?' he asked, puzzled.

'No, I don't!' Julie said defiantly. 'Of course I *do* love Andrew and getting engaged was terribly exciting but I don't want to settle down yet. If you're married, you just can't rush around and do mad things and have fun, can you?'

Yves smiled.

'Some married couples do just that, but perhaps you are right and this is not like Andrew.'

Julie's brows drew together thoughtfully.

'You know, Yves, I'm beginning to wonder if I am the right girl for Andrew after all. I know we have lots of interests in common but in character we aren't a bit alike. Andrew's so stable and I know I'm not.'

'And you think this is bad? Sometimes I think it is good for two people to be not alike. Andrew can make you perhaps the little more steady, no? And you can make him the little more gay.'

Julie relaxed, laughing again.

'I could listen to you for hours, Yves. Your English is awfully good really but you have the most fascinating accent. Let's not talk about Andrew and me. Tell me about yourself. You're not engaged, are you? Have you a girl friend? Dozens, I suppose!'

'You are, Mademoiselle Julie, the little bit *enfant terrible*. Such questions you should not ask. I do not have dozens of girl friends, though, as you seem to suppose. There is no girl with whom I am in love at this moment.'

'Then maybe there will be soon!' Julie countered. 'Maybe you'll fall for my little sister. Emma's a darling. I know she likes you but I'm afraid she's just the littlest bit in love with Andrew.'

'And you do not mind?' Yves asked, astounded.

'No, why should I? Emma has always adored Andrew and no one takes it seriously, least of all Andrew. I think he still thinks of her as a schoolgirl, which, of course, she still is.'

'But not here!' Yves said, placing his hand over his heart. 'I know she is not really quite grown up but at the same time, she is not a child no longer.'

Julie gave Yves a quick searching look.

'So you have noticed her!' she said with just the hint of irritation in her voice. The last thing in the world she sought was a serious flirtation with Yves and yet she wanted his admiration; the flattery of knowing he was attracted to her. That he should be interested in Emma, whom she had never once looked upon as a rival for any boy's attentions, aroused faint stirrings of jealousy.

'Julie, I think it is time we went to look for the others!' Yves said quietly. He felt out of his depth. Somehow his conversation with Julie had become much too quickly personal. He really did not wish to become involved with Julie, nor to upset Andrew whom he rather liked. At the same time, it was impossible not to feel the pull of Julie's attraction. He sensed that she found him attractive, too. It could become a dangerous situation — the more so since this young girl was obviously very impulsive and not very discreet.

'I don't want to go yet!' Julie said, looking at Yves from beneath her lashes in a way which excited him although he knew she was being deliberately provocative. 'I'd rather stay here talking to you.'

'All the same, I think it best we go. It is bad for you — and for me, too — to remain in such wet clothes for very long.'

Julie's eyes were full of mischief again.

'I think that's just an excuse!' she said. 'I think you're afraid to stay with me in case Andrew throws a fit when we get back!'

'Throws a fit?' Yves' question, diverted in spite of his intentions by her colloquialism.

'Gets angry with you!' Julie explained, laughing.

'You are a very naughty girl!' Yves said, smiling even as he reproved her. 'You would like it if this happened. But as you say, I would not.'

'Then you don't think I'm worth a row with Andrew?'

Yves shook his head.

'That is not the point. Love is a serious matter, Julie, and you should not treat it as a game.'

Once again, Julie was pouting.

'Now don't you start lecturing me, Yves!' she said. 'I don't want to take life seriously. Why should I at my age? If I feel like flirting with you, I shall — unless, of course, you object.'

This time Yves refused to be drawn. He knew very well that but for Andrew, he would have wanted nothing more than a holiday flirtation with this pretty English girl. But he was not going to let her know it if he could help it. He stood up, calling for his bill, and put a hand firmly under Julie's elbow.

'We are going back to the hotel!' he said. 'And you are to be especially nice to Andrew who is, no doubt, most upset.'

Julie tossed her head.

'Bother Andrew!' she said. 'He's spoiling all my fun.'

The waitress came over with the bill which Yves paid. They walked towards the door and as they did so, the door opened and Penny, together with Paul, rushed in, greeting Julie with cries of delight. They were followed by Emma, Lindy and lastly Andrew, who stood staring at Julie in amazement.

'Well, what on earth are you doing here?' he greeted her, too surprised to see her to be angry or otherwise.

Julie explained how they had had to take shelter and had come in for something hot to warm up as they were soaked through. At once, Andrew looked concerned.

'Then we'll skip our tea and I'll drive you both straight back to the hotel,' he said. 'You'll get double pneumonia hanging around like that.'

'Oh, don't be such a stuffy old thing!' Julie cried. 'You're worse than Mother. A bit of salt water won't hurt.'

Andrew's face flushed quickly at her criticism.

'Very well, then we will have tea. Sit down, Emma, Lindy, kids.'

Julie felt suddenly foolish. Andrew was perfectly right — it was silly to hang about too long in wet clothes and even if they left now, it would take at least half an hour to get across in the ferry and drive the five odd kilometres back to the hotel. Now she would have to wait while the family ate through a mound of cakes and drank hot chocolate. She quickly suppressed a shiver and sat down at an adjoining table.

Andrew ignored her. In none too good French, he ordered what everyone wanted as if Julie and Yves were not present. It fell to Emma to break the silence between the two tables, asking first Julie and then Yves about the sailing.

Julie felt increasingly annoyed. Andrew really was obtuse — deliberately. If he went on in this vein, she really would begin to think twice about their engagement. After all, she hadn't done anything he could reasonably object to. He was just making trouble.

'Do you know, at one point we very nearly capsized!' she told Emma in a voice intended for Andrew. Surely now he would look up at her anxiously, ask how it had happened. But Andrew did not turn his head. Penny and Paul burst into eager questions.

'Were you nearly drowned?'

'Did the boat begin to sink?'

She answered them with replies exaggerating the danger. Still Andrew appeared completely disinterested. Furious, Julie turned her attention back to Yves. He shook his head at her and whispered:

'Half you said is not true and now you fiancé will believe you and really have reason to be annoyed that I let you be in danger.'

'He couldn't care less if I did drown!' Julie whispered back. 'And if we didn't want that lift home, I'd jolly well go and leave him here.'

Paul came across to their table and began to tell Julie in detail about the car ferry which seemed to have fascinated him. It was pulled each way by heavy chains which were wound up on big cog wheels inside the ferry.

'You can see it working!' he said breathlessly. 'And, Julie, lots of the women wear fancy dress. Emma calls it National Costume. It's ever so funny. They have tall white hats and black shawls. Penny wants to buy a doll dressed like that.'

Julie nodded, not really listening. Paul went back to his own table. Andrew was now deep in conversation with Emma and Lindy.

'He's ignoring me on purpose!' Julie

told herself. 'Well, let him. Tonight I shall really give him something to be shirty about. I'll flirt with Yves and . . . and make him kiss me if I can. Then if I have to put up with Andrew in this mood, I'll know he has some justification.'

Yves, unaware of her trend of thought, but anxious to break the uncomfortable silence, spoke across Julie to Emma.

'Have you plans for this evening?' he asked politely. 'If not, I would be pleased if you would let me take you all into the cinema. I noticed in the paper this morning that there is an American film in Quimper. It will be spoken in French, of course, but it will have English sub-titles. Would you all come?'

Emma looked from Andrew to Julie and then at Lindy who was nodding her head enthusiastically. She would enjoy it, too.

'What do you think, Andrew?' she asked him.

'Let's go, Emma!' Lindy cried. And

Julie said firmly:

'I shall certainly go!'

'Then I shall come with you!' Andrew said, his voice over-loud and sarcastic. 'Since it seems that you aren't able to look after yourself.'

The deliberate reference to their sailing mishaps annoyed Julie still further. She met Andrew's smouldering eyes with a cold, unfriendly stare.

'Do as you please,' she said. 'It doesn't matter to me whether you come or not.'

Andrew's face turned a dull scarlet. But for the presence of the children, he would have continued the conversation a good deal further. But he restrained himself with a mammoth effort of self control. Watching him, Yves felt nothing but admiration for the slow, measured way in which he rose to his feet and beckoned the waitress to bring his bill. He admired Andrew's self control and the pride that forbade him making a scene in public. But at the same time, he could not help feeling that this was not the kind of restrained behaviour that would impress Julie. What she really needed was for Andrew to put her over his knee and spank her!

He glanced at Julie and saw she was looking at him with a slow, deliberate stare. As their eyes met, hers broke into a smile.

'I know!' she whispered. 'You've no need to tell me . . . ' she mimicked his accent admirably . . . 'I am a very naughty leetle girl.'

She saw by the smile on Yves' face that she had won him over; that his disapproval of her behaviour to Andrew was no longer of any importance.

'He's nice!' she told herself, and suddenly felt herself blushing. With Andrew, her fiancé, at the next table, she had no right to be thinking of Yves in this way; thinking of him as a highly attractive and likeable boy in whose company she might have a lot of fun. She must be crazy to think she would make him kiss her just to annoy Andrew. She loved Andrew and now she was his fiancé, she had no right to kiss anyone else but him.

She looked down at her hand, lying on the table, and realised that despite her promise to Andrew yesterday, she was still not wearing the sapphire ring.

7

But the visit to the cinema was not to take place for Andrew or Emma who were both suddenly taken ill at the hotel. At first, both sets of parents were extremely worried when without warning Andrew and Emma within a half hour developed violent stomach cramps and were very sick. However, Yves' parents were reassuring. It seemed that many tourists became ill in this way — perhaps due to the shell fish served in the hotel. By morning, Madame Courtelle said, both patients should be themselves again and there was little cause to worry.

Julie, filled with remorse, called in to see Andrew, who lay pale and wretched huddled up in bed.

'Darling, I'm so sorry!' she said. 'About this afternoon, too! Honestly, Andrew, I didn't mean to be so beastly!

Will you forgive me?'

He gave her a wan smile. It was typical of Julie to make such a handsome apology when really he had been as much to blame.

'Of course, we won't go to the film without you,' Julie went on as if she knew what was at the back of his mind. She gave him a quick mischievous smile. 'So you can relax and rest in peace!'

'Nonsense, of course you must go,' Andrew forced himself to reply. If Julie was prepared to give in, then the least he could do was to show that he trusted her. 'How is poor Emma?'

'About the same as you. I wonder why the rest of us didn't get ill? We all ate the crab at lunch — at least, I think so!'

'We probably ate the wrong part of it,' Andrew replied. 'Now beat it, Julie — I think I might very well be sick again and I'd rather you weren't here. Go and enjoy yourself. I mean it.'

Despite Andrew's approval to the

idea of them going to the cinema without him, Julie would have stayed at the hotel but for Emma's disapproving voice saying:

'Of course, you won't go now Lindy's called off, will you?'

Lindy had elected to stay behind and keep Emma company.

Julie felt a flash of irritation.

'Don't be silly, Emma. Of course I'd go with Yves alone, if I wanted to. In fact, Andrew told me to go.'

'Then all the more reason why you shouldn't!' Emma said weakly. 'You know it would only make him miserable.'

'Oh, for goodness' sake!' Julie flared. 'I'm getting fed up with the way you go on about Andrew. He's my business, not yours, although it's beginning to look very much as if you've more than a sisterly interest in him. Anyway, I thought you liked Yves.'

'Of course I do!' Emma was relieved to get off the subject of Andrew. 'It's just that . . . well, you are *engaged* and . . . ' She broke off, suddenly near to tears. 'You're quite right, it isn't any of my business.'

Julie felt the implied criticism of the way she treated Andrew and because her heart told her it was warranted, she reacted the more violently to it.

'No, it isn't your business!' she reiterated. 'And I'm sorry if you don't approve, little sister, but I'm going to the film with Yves, *on my own*, whether you like it or not.'

She flounced out of Emma's room and head high, went down to the lobby where Yves was sitting playing Happy Families with the younger children. She felt miserable and not a little guilty at the way she had spoken to Emma, especially when Emma was obviously feeling as rotten as Andrew. If only they would all leave her alone and let her lead her life in her own way. Maybe she had been silly to rush into an engagement with Andrew. It had been an impulsive decision — made on the spur of the moment when he suddenly produced the ring at her party. Somehow, getting engaged had seemed exactly the right thing to do at that moment. But it hadn't seemed right since! She didn't want her freedom of action curtailed. She didn't want to *settle* down. Life was full of adventure and she wanted to savour every moment of it. Of course she did love Andrew, but instead of having more fun together since their engagement, they'd had far less with Andrew taciturn and jealous and possessive.

Yves looked up at her as the game finished.

'You wish to play, too?' he asked.

Julie tossed her head.

'Isn't it time we were going?' she asked, her voice brittle.

'Going? But I thought that since the others are ill, we do not go after all? Lindy told me she stay to look after Emma and . . . '

'Is it too much trouble to take *just me*?'

She was looking at him with those

fantastic blue eyes flashing a challenge. Yves stared back, half uneasy, half excited by what he read there. Danger, yes! It would perhaps be best not to go, yet . . .

'It is as you wish,' he said formally. 'If you like to go, then I take you.'

Now that she had won her point, Julie was no longer sure she wanted to go. Despite everything she had said to Emma, her conscience bothered her about poor Andrew, lying ill upstairs. However, she could hardly back out now without losing face all round and not least in Yves' eyes, too.

Yves drove her in his parents' Citroën. He made no attempt to break the silence Julie had maintained since they got into the car. He sensed her uneasiness of spirit and decided to let her work out her own mood in her own time. After ten minutes, she said:

'I suppose you think I'm behaving very badly, too!' She sounded like a defiant child. She did not see the smile that touched the corners of Yves' mouth.

'Not very — just a leetle!' he agreed.

Julie gave a long sigh.

'But at least you don't go on at me about it,' she said.

'It is hardly my business — right word, yes? — to tell you how to behave,' Yves replied caustically. 'But if you wish my opinion, I am quite willing to give it to you.'

Julie's red mouth was pouting.

'Go on then. I might as well have it from you, too.'

'Then I will tell you that if you were my fiancée, I would do one of two things — I would decide that you did not love me and break off the engagement; or I would decide that you were a most naughtee girl and put you over my knee and spank you very hard.'

Julie's mood changed and suddenly she laughed.

'You wouldn't dare!' she said. 'For one thing, I'm probably as strong as you. Anyway, I was always told the French men were so gallant with girls. It wouldn't be very gallant to spank me!'

'No, but it is what you need, Mademoiselle Julie. I think you like to play with the fire, no? It is always the dangerous game. You have not thought that in your little affair with Andrew you have given me a rôle to play, too? Suppose I were to accept this rôle and play the part of 'the other man'!'

This time Julie laughed aloud.

'Well, it is just what you are doing, isn't it?' she teased. 'After all, here we are alone in a car miles from everyone. For all Andrew and Emma know, you might very well be seducing me at this moment.'

'And you are not afraid that I might do just this?'

'You? Of course not! You're much too nice!'

Yves sighed.

'You are very young, Julie. Perhaps most of the time, this innocence of yours can protect you, but not always. You are very attractive and you know how to provoke a man, excite him. You do this deliberately and yet you are not prepared to take the consequences. Perhaps it would be a good lesson for you if I showed you what these consequences could be. After all, what do you know of me? Nothing! A few days ago we had not met. Our parents do not know each other. I might be a man of the worst type who would take advantage of you in these circumstances.'

Julie snuggled back against the seat, her eyes sparkling with amusement. There was not the slightest fear in her.

'I just *know* you aren't like that!' she cried.

To her surprise Yves suddenly put his foot on the brake and drew into the side of the road. She barely had time to wonder if something had gone wrong with the car before he switched off the headlights and turned and took her in his arms. She opened her mouth to speak but his mouth came down on hers hard. She struggled for a moment but his lips held hers and she forgot the sudden fear that had risen to her mind as she felt the swift uprising of very different emotions charging though her body.

She began to return his kiss, her heart pounding, her eyes closed, her whole being terribly aware of the man in whose arms she was now almost half lying.

Then, as suddenly as he had commenced, he stopped kissing her and thrust her away from him. For a moment, she sat perfectly still, every nerve in her body throbbing against this abrupt ending. She wanted that kiss to go on for ever; to sweep her to even greater sensations of pleasure and delight. She didn't understand anything — only that she wanted him to take her back in his arms again.

Yves spoke first. In a small, hard voice, he said:

'I'm sorry. I shouldn't have done that. I just meant to teach you a lesson but . . . '

She stared at him in the near darkness, her eyes enormous.

127

'A lesson?' she repeated stupidly.

'Yes! You cannot flirt with a man, deliberately provoke his interest in you and not expect a response. I thought I would frighten you just a little — make you believe just for a moment that I might — how do you say? — take advantage of you? I did not mean . . . '

He broke off, unsure how to explain his own behaviour. When he had decided to kiss her, it had indeed been merely to show her that her actions could be misconstrued — not by him, but by other men with whom she might decide to play the same dangerous game of flirtation. He had not reckoned on his own weaknesses! Julie was a very desirable and beautiful girl. He'd been carried away and it had taken a great effort of will not to keep her there in his arms, warm, responsive, passionate and terribly attractive. The pretended seduction might all too easily have ceased to be a pretence.

'I don't understand!' The tone of Julie's voice was very different now.

Gone was the self-assurance, the challenge, the coquetry. It sounded terribly young, distressed, much more like Emma's.

She was frightened — not because she thought Yves would try to seduce her, but because he had somehow managed to arouse in her emotions she'd never known before. In all the times she had kissed Andrew, she had never experienced this terrible longing for something more. Andrew was always so restrained. In Yves' kiss there had been no restraint. And her body had lit to his touch like a torch. Even now, she was still trembling.

'You were . . . playing a game with me?' she asked hesitantly.

Yves' voice was rough.

'I was! But the game got a little out of the hand. That is what I meant, Julie. Sex is not something to play with. In a man it is a serious thing and so it should be for a woman, too.'

'Oh, sex!' She tried to regain some of her old flippancy but knew, even as she spoke, that she sounded childish and young. The thought that Yves might be laughing at her brought the colour rushing to her cheeks. 'That's all you men ever think of!' she cried. 'You're all the same.'

Yves did not respond to this as Andrew would have. Instead of trying to defend himself, he said quietly:

'And are you so different, Julie? Were you not as ready for sex as I, too, just now?'

Again the colour flared in her cheeks so that she was glad of the darkness. She knew that he already knew the answer. For the first time in her life, she had been deeply sexually stirred and she was afraid of herself more than of the man beside her. But she feared him, too. He seemed to understand her far too well.

'You think I was *serious* just now?' She gave a scornful laugh. 'Why, I've been much further than that with other boys and still not succumbed. You must think I'm an inexperienced little fool if you think a mere kiss or two could affect me.'

Slowly Yves drew out a packet of cigarettes and lit one. The smell of the French tobacco drifted across to Julie, unfamiliar and somehow unnerving. She wondered what he was thinking and half regretted her last remarks.

Yves smoked in silence. Now he, too, was unsure of himself. He had been convinced that Julie was little more than an inexperienced schoolgirl. He knew her parents, guessed she had been strictly brought up. Now he wasn't sure. She was, after all, English and he knew little of English girls. He'd read that promiscuity was the order of the day amongst English teenagers but he had assumed that the Prescotts did not come into this category. In France, the young girls of good family were still carefully guarded and he had taken it for granted that Julie was of this type. Her last words refuted it. If he believed her, and why should she lie about such a thing, she was not innocent after all.

What a fool she must be thinking him!

He bit his lip uneasily. He was out of his depth.

'Well, haven't you anything to say?' Julie asked, unable to bear the silence any longer.

'Only that I'm sorry. I shouldn't have kissed you.'

She was suddenly even more annoyed with him. Why apologise for a kiss? Anyone would think they'd committed a crime.

She said as much in a tight little voice. Then added:

'I suppose you'll bring Andrew into this in a minute. You shouldn't have kissed me because I'm engaged. Is that it?'

'That's part of it. Are you really in love with him, Julie?'

'Well, that's my business, not yours!' Julie said. '*I'm* not sorry and it seems to me you're making a mountain out of a silly little molehill. The way you're apologising makes one harmless little kiss into an act of indencency or something . . . ' she added lamely.

'Indecency?' To her embarrassment, the word was unfamiliar to him. She was forced to elaborate.

'Well, as if we'd done something worse!' In the darkness she was blushing and she felt a momentary sympathy with poor little Emma, who often blushed. Julie never did — as a rule.

Yves stayed silent, smoking his cigarette and staring out of the windscreen, his free hand lying on the wheel.

To her surprise, when he next spoke, his voice was softer, gentle.

'You have not even been with a man, have you, Julie?'

It was more a statement of fact than a question but as if some demon inside her were prompting her, she gave a hard little laugh and said in a brittle voice:

'Whatever makes you jump to that conclusion? Was my kissing so inadequate?'

She heard Yves' quick indrawn

breath, almost as if he were shocked at her reply and immediately wished it unsaid. But now she was too proud to withdraw the implication. She said: 'Don't engaged couples do *that* in France?'

'Sometimes!'

'Well, what makes you think I'm so inexperienced?'

Yves threw his cigarette end out of the window and turning, laid his hand over Julie's.

'Perhaps because you are so much anxious to prove me wrong, to prove to me that you are not a virgin. It is more usual for a girl to want to prove that she is, if in fact, she is not. Please let us discontinue this conversation, Julie. We shall now almost certainly be too late for the cinema. Maybe we should returned to the hotel?'

Julie bit her lip. Nothing seemed to be turning out right. Somehow, she and Yves, whom she had liked, were almost quarrelling. It was as if she couldn't have a normal relationship with anyone

— especially Andrew. The thought of Andrew lying ill in bed and trusting her, made her feel even more unhappy. She had landed herself in a situation she did not know how to handle. She wasn't sure about anything any more — especially her own feelings. Why, as Yves suggested, should she have wanted to make out she lived a promiscuous life: and especially since she had never once in her life felt tempted to do anything really serious with Andrew. The only time she had really been tempted to misbehave was just now — with Yves! And that did not make sense since it was Andrew she loved.

She felt tears stinging her eyes — tears that were part frustration, part confusion. She had never felt so young and incapable and confused.

'I suppose you dislike me now!' she cried.

'On the contrary, I like you a little too much,' Yves said quietly. 'I think you are in a muddle, Julie, and it was wrong of me to add to your confusion.

It is not so easy to grow up and maybe from the girl to the woman is more harder than from the boy to the man. It is wrong that I should make more the muddle in your mind. Maybe it is for the best if I tell my parents I wish to leave the hotel tomorrow. I do not have to give a reason — merely to say I wish for something more gay. They will do as I wish.'

'Oh, no, Yves!' The plea came before she could stop it. Again a blush spread over her face. 'Please don't do that. There is no need. I'm not in the least confused. At least, not by you. I admit I'm not absolutely sure about my engagement to Andrew but that isn't your fault. And anyway, if I'm not really in love with Andrew after all, surely it's better for both of us if I find out now?'

She wasn't sure why she wanted him to stay. She knew that the whole holiday would be spoilt for her if he went.

'I shall think about it tonight!' Yves said. 'But one thing I am sure of, Julie — I must be just your friend — no more kissing. That is not right when you are fiancée. Understood?'

She felt herself relax, confident now that he didn't really want to leave; that he did still like her. It was important that he should like her.

'Understood!' she said. And with one of her swift changes of mood, she was suddenly on top of the world again. Her eyes lost their sombre thoughtfulness and sparkled dangerously. 'It's a pity, though, isn't it? About the kissing. I rather enjoyed it!'

Yves made no reply. He restarted the engine and pulled the car back onto the road. He had no intention of revealing to Julie just how much he had enjoyed that kiss, too.

8

It was a perfect afternoon — the sun full of warmth and only a light breeze blowing in from the Atlantic. Everyone but Emma and Andrew had gone down to the beach. The two invalids sat in the hotel garden, still weak from last night's upset, two convalescents not yet up to bathing and beach games.

They were each silent, lost in thought. Emma was content just to lie with her eyes shut, knowing that Andrew was there beside her. She could smell the salt in the wind; hear the slap of the water against the jetty and the occasional shrill call of the gulls. She was perfectly happy and savouring every moment of it. It was worth yesterday's acute discomfort to have Andrew to herself for a whole afternoon.

Andrew, too, was moderately happy.

Julie, though she had in the end gone down to the beach with the others rather than stay here with Emma and himself, had nevertheless gone off wearing her ring. She had put it on this morning without him having to repeat his request to her to do so. Moreover, she seemed to be particularly loving when she had sat beside him in the deck chair this morning where Emma now lay half asleep. Twice she had called him 'darling' and she'd made no move to withdraw her hand when he'd reached over and taken possession of it.

True she had not been very communicative about last night's cinema trip with Yves but he rather fancied she might have quarrelled with the French boy because she had deliberately avoided him since breakfast; and when Yves had announced that he was going sailing, she had said firmly that she was spending the morning in the garden with him, Andrew, and there'd been no suggestion of her going sailing. He felt sure Julie was trying to make amends;

to show him in her own way that she really did love him and hated their quarrels as much as he did.

If he had been disappointed that she did not wish to spend the afternoon with him as well, he had managed to hide it from her. It wasn't fair to restrict her to an afternoon of inactivity as well as a whole morning. Julie was always so full of energy! He could sense her restlessness as it neared lunch time and knew that even as she listened to what he was saying, half of her had one ear listening for the lunch gong.

He loved her even though he guessed her impatience to be away from him. But her goodbye kiss before she left for the beach with the family, more than made up for any small hurt at her going. It was somehow deeper, with more real feeling behind it. Weak though he was still feeling after last night's mild bout of food poisoning, he had wanted to make love to her more than ever before. It was as if she had meant her kiss to be different. Knowing

Julie in the past, he couldn't quite bring himself to believe that she was being deliberately provocative for she usually shied away from sex like a young colt! All the same, the kiss had been different, lingering, sensual, stirring up emotions in him he usually tried hard to quash in Julie's company. He was afraid of the force of his own passionate need of her when he held her in his arms. If he once let go of even a small part of his self-control, he knew that he would lose all restraint and he had far too much respect for her to want that!

'Isn't it peaceful, Andrew?'

Emma's soft voice beside him brought his thoughts back to the present. He turned and looked at her, lying with dark lashes on those soft apricot-coloured cheeks, the clear young line of her profile outlined against the dark green of the trees beyond. He was surprised to find himself suddenly realising that Emma was no longer a child. The chubby curves of the schoolgirl had, it seemed overnight, given way to the more sculptured lines of a woman. One day she was going to be very beautiful — perhaps in the strict sense more beautiful than Julie.

Emma opened her eyes and saw him staring at her and the colour rose to her cheeks. She smiled at him shyly.

'Penny for them!' she said, wanting to break the silence.

Andrew smiled back.

'They're really worth more than that. I was thinking that you're growing very pretty, Emma, and that one day you'll outshine even Julie. There now, agree they're worth more than sixpence.'

'They're worth more than a king's ransom!' Emma thought, pleasure coursing through her whole body. Even Andrew's qualified 'one day' couldn't mar the compliment. Yet at the same time, she felt guilty at knowing such happiness. She must not let herself love Andrew. One day soon he would be Julie's husband — her brother-in-law. She could not bear the thought.

Andrew saw the pallor steal back into her face and said solicitously:

'You feeling okay, Emma? Sun not too much for you?'

'No, I'm fine!' She closed her eyes again afraid lest they should reveal the extent of her love for him. Being in love was terrible! A mixture of ecstasy and pain. Such little things could bring such vast joy and yet equally small things could bring pain. She had been so hurt for Andrew last night when Julie went off to the film with Yves. It had seemed such a cruel selfish action on her sister's part when Andrew lay ill and unable to defend himself.

Emma was too honest to be able to transfer her anger at Julie to anger at Yves. She knew, none better, her sister's strong determined nature and guessed that it was at her persuasion rather than Yves' insistence that they'd gone off together last night after all. Yves had proved himself thoughtful and kind and Emma liked him. He had taken the trouble to sit with her for ten minutes after breakfast, enquiring about her health, as if he really minded whether she was better or not. He had an attractive personality and she could see only too well what Julie found to like in him. But Julie had no right to find him attractive. She longed to say to Yves:

'Don't tempt her, Yves. She belongs to Andrew. If you keep out of her way, she can't hurt Andrew!' But of course, she couldn't say any such thing and Yves would probably think she was mad if she did.

She thought of them all on the beach — building another 'Buckingham Palace' perhaps, with Julie and Yves kneeling side by side laughing and enjoying themselves. It wasn't fair! But at least Andrew didn't seem perturbed at the thought if it had even crossed his mind. She would have expected him to be terribly jealous.

Madame, the hotel proprietor, brought out a tray of what she called 'English tea' for the two invalids. In fact, tea consisted of two tiny muslin teabags floating in hot water with a slice of lemon on top. Emma and Andrew grimaced at each other after Madame had gone but when they came to drink the tea, it turned out to be far more refreshing and pleasant to their upset stomachs than strong tea with milk and sugar.

Not long after, Emma's parents returned with the younger children. Mrs. Prescott told them that Julie and Yves were walking home round the rocks. They'd estimated it would take them little over an hour and both wanted the exercise.

'Yes, Julie and I walked home yesterday morning,' Andrew said. He was suddenly depressed. Julie was obviously in no hurry to get back to him. He tried to still the murmurings of jealousy once more rousing in him. Yesterday Julie had stopped on the deserted beach to kiss him. Suppose . . .

'Let's go in, Andrew!' Emma's voice broke in on his thoughts. 'It's getting chilly all of a sudden.'

'I think I'll take a short walk,' Andrew said on impulse. 'I might wander round the rocks and meet them. I'm feeling miles better — a bit of exercise won't hurt me.'

It was on the tip of Emma's tongue to ask if she could go too but something in the set expression of Andrew's mouth forbade her suggesting it.

'I'll see you later then,' she said as casually as she could. But as she walked slowly into the hotel, all her happiness of a moment ago had vanished and in its place was a chill foreboding.

★　★　★

It had been Julie's idea to walk back to the hotel. At first Yves had declined, saying it was too hot to walk but something in the quick rise of Julie's eyebrows — the question in her eyes — had challenged him. It was as if she were saying to him:

'Surely you're not afraid of me?'

All afternoon she had been subconsciously if not consciously provoking him. Mostly it was simple childish teasing — 'Race you to the water' 'I can swim faster than you!' But lying in the sand after their swim, he had been forced to awareness of the golden brown body in its brief bikini stretched out beside him, near enough for him to touch her with the merest movement of his body. She lay on her side staring at him, her eyes large, round, wide open, her lashes and hair still wet with the salt water, her skin shining with droplets.

He tried to ignore her but it was impossible. Either she threw a handful of warm sand onto his stomach or she was asking him to rub oil onto her back and shoulders where she could not reach.

Once he said:

'You are playing with fire, Julie!' But she only laughed and told him not to be an old silly — that he was getting as stuffy as Andrew.

Despite what she had told him in the car, he was still fairly sure she was innocent. Yet now and again he surprised a look in her eyes that left him deeply disturbed. Had he met her in different circumstances, he would not have hesitated to answer that look. But he liked her family — her parents had obviously accepted him as part of the group and trusted him. He liked Andrew, too, though he was beginning to think him a bit of a fool the way he was treating Julie. She needed someone to take her in hand and Andrew was far too nice to her in Yves' opinion. No, he could not do anything that would upset or hurt her family; anything that later he would feel ashamed about. It was simply that he was not made of stone and Julie was behaving in such a way as to invite him to take friendship a stage further.

They walked slowly along the beach, bare feet leaving prints in the soft wet sand. For a little while, neither spoke. Then Julie said:

'I stayed awake a long time last night — thinking. I've reached a conclusion. I'm not in love with Andrew the way I ought to be if I'm going to marry him.

I think I ought to break our engagement.'

Yves stared down at her in dismay.

'But that is madness, Julie. Why? What reason have you for such a serious decision?'

Julie tossed her head.

'Because of the way I felt when you kissed me. I'm being quite frank about it and if you're shocked I can't help it. The fact is, I liked you kissing me. Enough said?'

'No, it is not enough!' Yves said, quickening his pace in agitation without realising it. 'You cannot break your engagement because of one kiss — that is too absurd!'

'No it isn't!' Julie said calmly. 'It isn't so much the kiss as the way I enjoyed it. Oh, I'm not trying to say I've fallen in love with you. That would be silly. But I find you very attractive and I think you find me attractive and I know I wish Andrew weren't here — then we'd be free to have lots of fun together.'

'Fun!' Yves stopped dead in his tracks and stared at her. 'This I do not understand, Julie. Marriage is a very serious business — an engagement also. Yet you talk of 'fun'.'

'There, that's exactly it!' Julie said triumphantly. 'It shows I'm not ready for marriage. I just want fun. Right now I wish you'd kiss me again.'

He saw laughter in her eyes but desire, too, and he turned away quickly, not trusting himself to stay unmoved by her candid request. Really, this girl was an enigma. It could be said she was throwing herself at him and yet her manner of doing so was so immature that he simply could not look at her as he might any girl who was 'easy-to-get'.

'It is natural for young men and women to find each other attractive,' he said as he might have spoken to Emma. 'You should not let this confuse you about love, Julie.'

Julie gave her bare shoulders a slight shrug.

'You say that but of course I'm confused. Surely I should be attracted to Andrew the way I am to you? I

150

suppose I shouldn't say that, but why pretend? *You* find *me* attractive, don't you?'

'Yes! Who wouldn't? But that is of little importance, Julie. What you feel in your heart for Andrew is something much more. Also you have known him a long time whereas between us it is new and therefore exciting.'

Julie gave him a mischievous little smile.

'Now, you've admitted it's exciting. That's what I mean, Yves. It isn't exciting with Andrew. Oh, we kiss and hold hands and tell each other how much we love each other but it's certainly never kept me awake at night. Even Emma who knows nothing about love says that I couldn't be so casual about Andrew if I really loved him.'

'Emma is not so ignorant as you might suppose, Julie. There are times, and this is one of them, when I think she knows a great deal more about life than you do — that she is more grown-up. I'm sorry for your Andrew. I think he has quite a problem on his hands.'

Julie sighed.

'I don't see why you should be sorry for him. I was very nice to him this morning. I even wore . . . oh, my goodness!' She broke off with a cry, the fingers of one hand feverishly searching for the sapphire ring. 'Oh, Yves, it's gone. I've lost it. Oh, how terrible!'

She turned to face the way they had come and shaded her hand to her eyes as if she might see the ring lying back in the far distant sand. Her face was white and shocked.

'Calm yourself!' Yves said. 'It cannot be lost. You did not wear your ring for swimming, of that I am sure. I remember that you took it off before we ran to the water, no?'

Julie had already started walking back along the beach, and Yves quickened his steps to keep pace with her.

'Yes, I took it off, you're quite right. I put it on my towel. When we came out

I forgot about it. Oh, how terrible of me. I shouldn't have worn it. I told Andrew I shouldn't wear it on the beach. I just knew something awful like this would happen. He'll never forgive me. I'll never forgive myself . . . '

She started to run, Yves following with a slight frown on his forehead. Julie really was an enigma. Her behaviour now was that of someone desperate to recover a treasured object. Was it just the ring she valued, or was she really concerned for Andrew after all? Whatever the reason, he said a silent prayer to St. Anthony, patron saint who helped to find lost objects, to recover this one.

But although they searched the sand for a whole hour, there was absolutely no trace of the ring. Julie was nearly in tears.

'We might as well be looking for a needle in the proverbial haystack!' she cried, sitting back on her heels and letting the sand drift through her fingers. 'We'll never find it. When Lindy took my towel it must have rolled off and become buried. Yves, *how* am I going to tell Andrew? He'll never forgive me — never!'

Her eyes were full of tears and to comfort her, Yves put his arm round her shoulders and she leant against him, utterly miserable and not a little frightened. It seemed crazy now that she could have been talking only a short while ago about breaking off her engagement to Andrew. She did love him. The last thing in the world she wanted was to hurt him and he was so proud of the ring; so proud to see her wearing it. She didn't deserve anyone like Andrew. He was far too good for her. It served her right that Fate should punish her in this way. It must be a kind of retribution for the way she had been carrying on with Yves.

Tears that were partly caused by genuine worry and partly by self-pity, rolled down her cheeks. Yves who had no handkerchief, wiped them away with his forefinger.

'We must go back, Julie. It's after six and they'll all be worrying about us. Maybe somehow the ring became attached to the towel and Lindy has it safely. Try not to worry. When we get back to the hotel, we shall no doubt find it safe and . . . '

'I thought you were supposed to be walking back to the hotel!'

They looked up, Julie's face still streaked with sandy tears, to find Andrew, white and shaking, standing over them. He had not heard Yves' words — only seen the two of them crouching in the sand, Julie's face against the French boy's. All the pent-up jealousy of the last few days flared to the surface and he had nearly hit Yves as he approached them. Only the fact that Yves had his back to him prevented him. You couldn't hit a chap in the back!

Julie, shocked, burst into tears. Yves stood up and faced Andrew.

'We started back but . . . ' he gave Julie a quick look . . . 'but then Julie

155

found her ring was missing and we came back to search for it!'

'A good excuse . . . ' Andrew began furiously, when the meaning of Yves' words hit him. 'You've lost my ring?' he asked Julie as if he could not believe it. 'But you can't lose it — it's our engagement ring.'

'Oh, Andrew!' Julie sobbed. 'I'm so sorry!'

'Sorry!' Andrew was even whiter than before. 'You sit there and say you're sorry. I suppose you were mucking around with Yves and it just fell off! Well, now it's off it can stay off. It's perfectly clear to me you don't love me and never did. You never really wanted to get engaged to me, did you? But at least I believed you wanted the ring. Now I know you didn't care about that either!'

He knew he was being childish but he couldn't stop himself. The double shock of finding out what had happened on top of the thoughts that had been going through his mind all the long hour's walk to find them, coming on top of his recent illness, were proving too much.

'Crying won't find it!' he said bitterly, scornfully to Julie. 'Anyway, I wouldn't bother to look if I were you. You can stay here and smooch with your boy friend if you want to but I'm going home.'

'Andrew!' Julie jumped up and ran after him as he began to walk away. 'Andrew, listen, please listen. I do mind . . . I mind terribly. I loved my ring even more than you did. Andrew . . . '

But he continued walking, angrily brushing her hand off his arm as if it were an annoying fly.

Julie stopped, her mouth twisting into a hard, stubborn line, her eyes hurt. Slowly Yves came to her.

'You should go after him, Julie,' he said. 'He is very upset. You must make him see that you do love him.'

'Love him!' Julie repeated in a high, shrill voice. 'I'll never love him again. He must have *seen* how upset I was. He knows I never cry. I never, never cry . . . ' Suddenly she *was* crying, but she didn't seem to know it. 'He just wanted to hurt me because I lost the beastly ring. Well, I'm glad I lost it. Yes, I am, I'm glad. It serves him right. I hate him, I hate him.'

'And you love him,' Yves said but she did not hear him. 'Come, Julie!' He took her arm and began to walk her along the beach, the tears still streaming down her face. 'I do not want to make matters harder for you but, as your friend, and this I would like to be, I must warn you again not to play games. Losing the ring is an accident you cannot help, but losing the man you love — that would be very silly and I will not help you to do it.'

'Don't you dare say I love him. Don't you dare!' Julie all but shouted. But Yves only smiled.

Even if Andrew had not understood, he had seen for himself just how genuine was Julie's concern for the lost ring.

9

Lindy looked at Emma anxiously.

'Whatever happens, it won't affect our friendship, will it, Emma?' she asked, her eyes wide with genuine worry.

'Of course not, Lindy!' Emma said, stifling a half sigh. Lindy's attitude seemed so childish. Whatever the outcome of the quarrel between her friend's brother and her own sister it could not have any possible bearing on whether she and Lindy stayed friends. 'It's not our business,' she added quietly.

Lindy rolled over on her back and lay with her arms behind her head, staring up at the ceiling.

'I know that, but if we were to take sides ... well ... ' she paused significantly ... 'Well, you'd naturally side with Julie and I'd side with Andy and then next thing you and I would be quarrelling, too.'

'Then we'd best keep our thoughts to ourselves,' said Emma. It was only natural that Lindy would suppose she'd side with Julie but then Lindy hadn't the slightest idea that she was in love with Andrew and that over this, if not in a lot of other ways, too, she was definitely on his side. She'd never forget Andrew's white, shocked face as he came striding back into the hotel. Julie, looking slightly sulky, and Yves, rather embarrassed, were not far behind him. Andrew had gone straight up to his room and locked his door. Yves had disappeared in search of his parents and Emma and Lindy were the only two members of the family to hear Julie's outburst. She'd lost her engagement ring and Andrew was furious; he seemed to think she'd lost it deliber-ately and refused to talk to her. He was being childish and absurd and if he didn't want to know how desperately worried she herself was about the ring, then she wasn't going to force him to listen. Let him sulk. Maybe he was just using the lost ring as an excuse for breaking an engagement that was beginning to look more and more like a mistake.

But although Julie was flushed and angry, Emma knew her sister well enough to realise that she was upset, too; and genuinely worried about the ring because she went straight off in search of the younger children to see if by any chance, it could have been amongst their beach gear. Emma didn't doubt that Julie regretted losing the ring. It was obviously as much a shock to her as to any of them. Even Penny and Paul were upset and volunteered to go back to the beach to look for it. At first Julie seemed half inclined to return with them. With Lindy and Emma helping, they might just be lucky and find it. But the grown-ups who had now heard of the disaster, felt there was little to be served by trying to find the ring at this late hour. If it had been easily visible, Julie and Yves would have seen it when first they returned to the spot where it was missing. If it had been buried beneath the sand, then the chances of anyone finding it were so remote it didn't warrant a search party at this time of the evening. Julie and Yves had been sitting above the tide line. Tomorrow morning the whole family could make up a search party and perhaps one of them would unearth it or see it glinting in the sunshine. If not, Andrew would just have to put in a claim on his insurance and buy another one.

'Of course, it *may* turn up!' Lindy was saying. 'But I think we should have gone to look for it right away. After all, anyone down on the beach early tomorrow might find it and keep it. Personally, I think if Andrew does get it back, he'd be a fool to return it to Julie . . . ' She broke off, looking anxiously at Emma to see if her friend was angry. But Emma only said:

'I think he's still in love with her,

Lindy. Otherwise he wouldn't be so terribly upset.'

'Well, the ring was expensive!' Lindy argued.

'I don't think it is the cost he's worried about,' Emma defended Andrew without thinking.

Lindy sat up and swung her legs off the bed.

'Must be nearly supper time and I'm starving,' she changed the subject. 'Coming down to the dining room, Emma?'

The older girl shook her head.

'I still don't feel up to eating much,' she confessed. 'You go on, Lindy. I'll see you later.'

'Shall I bring you something — soup for instance?'

'No, I don't want anything — honestly.'

Lindy ran a comb through her hair and with a friendly wave to Emma, disappeared from the room. Emma lay quietly thinking. The more she considered the rift between Andrew and Julie, the more serious it seemed. She felt sure that unless the ring were found, nothing could come right for them. In a way, it was Andrew's fault for insisting that Julie wore her ring on the beach; but Julie was partly to blame. She must have been unusually careless to lose anything so valuable.

The plain fact emerged. The ring must be found.

Suddenly Emma made up her mind to go and search for it herself. It was still not quite dark. Although the sun had long since set and the sky was grey and cloudy, full darkness would not come for another hour at least. If she hurried, she could perhaps have a quarter of an hour left in which to look; longer if she took the big torch from her parents' car.

Emma had no sooner conceived the idea than she was off the bed, pulling on jeans and a couple of warm jerseys and canvas shoes. This was something concrete she could do for Andrew. She'd often imagined being able to be of service to him in some spectacular kind of way, aware that her thoughts were pure schoolgirl romanticism and not really believing there'd ever be a chance to save his life or nurse him through a dangerous illness! Finding the ring was not quite in that category but he would be immensely pleased. If everything then came right between him and Julie, it would be because of her, Emma. Andrew would realise it and be so grateful . . .

Knowing that her parents would try to prevent her going out in the cool evening air after her recent bout of food-poisoning, Emma waited until the families were in the dining room before she slipped quietly out of the hotel by the side door. She knew just which part of the beach to make for. Julie had told her they had been at the same place where the three of them had built the first 'Buckingham Palace' with Yves.

A couple of young fishermen tying up their boat whistled and grinned at Emma as she hurried past them. She blushed, aware that she was alone and must seem an object of curiosity at this time of night. She was glad when she had put distance between herself and them and could not hear their rough patois and laughter, for she was sure they had been discussing her; perhaps even debating whether or not to follow her.

She began to wish she had asked Lindy to accompany her but at the same time, knew that this was something she preferred to do on her own. She couldn't have explained to Lindy the strange compulsion to go — certainly not without revealing how deeply she felt for Andrew.

She was now past the rocks where the younger ones went crabbing, and had reached the sand dunes. In the half light, they were vague dark shapes. From time to time there seemed to be movement among them, as if someone were walking parallel with her but trying to keep out of sight.

She shivered, trying to still her fear. She was sure the two young fishermen were not following her — why should they? And no one else was likely to be down on the beach at this time.

She hurried on, forcing herself not to glance towards the dunes. Her legs ached and she realised that she was not yet fully over her upset. It had left her weaker than she had imagined. She shivered again, and wished she had added an anorak to her two jerseys. A chill breeze was coming off the water, whipping her cheeks and bringing tears to her eyes.

It seemed hours before she reached 'Buckingham Palace', although a glance at her watch showed her it had taken her only forty minutes to get there. Hurriedly she knelt down and began to search. Only then, as her hands wandered helplessly across the yards and yards of cold coarse sand did she realise just how absurd her actions were. How could she hope to find one tiny little ring in all this vast space? She must have been crazy ever to imagine she might find it. Yet still she remained on her knees, now using the torch in the hope that its beam of light would reflect off the sapphire stone.

She was so engrossed in what she was doing, she did not hear the footsteps approaching across the sand; did not know there was a man standing over her, staring down at her, until she heard his voice saying:

'Come on home, Emma. It's no use.'

'Andrew!'

He knelt down in the sand beside her and took the torch from her hands. For a moment, he shone the light into her face and then switched the torch off.

'It's no use,' he said again. 'I'm afraid it's really lost.'

Something in the hopeless tone of his voice aroused her from the first shock of hearing him in so unnerving and unexpected a manner.

'Oh, Andrew, I thought I might be lucky and come across it. It has to be here somewhere, doesn't it? Maybe if we look a bit longer . . . '

'No!' His voice was rough. 'It's lost and I'm not even sure I care. Julie doesn't seem to mind so why should I? *She* didn't come out here to look for it tonight. Yet you, Emma . . . ' He broke off as if he didn't himself enjoy hearing what he had to say.

Emma stood up, brushing the hair out of her eyes with hands that were covered with sand.

'Julie does care. She was terribly upset about it. But she has a lot of common sense — much more than I have — and she must have realised it would be useless trying to find it in the dark.'

'Yet you came — just in case!' The words seemed to be wrung up from somewhere deep inside him. She knew that in some way, her being here hurt him more than if she had not come.

'I'm sorry!' she said helplessly.

'Well, don't be!' He took her arm and began to walk her up the beach to the far side of the sand dunes where he had parked the car. He did not speak until they were inside the car. He made no move to switch on the engine but pulled out a packet of cigarettes and lit one before saying:

'When I saw you down there just now, on your hands and knees, looking, I was crazy enough to imagine that it was Julie. I'd been very hurt and angry with her but at that moment, I was willing to forgive everything. It was enough that she was here, alone in the dark, trying to make amends. I was going to tell her it didn't matter; that it was my fault anyway, for asking her to wear the ring all the time; that I loved her and that I knew she loved me and the ring was unimportant. Then . . . '

'Then you found me instead!' Emma could almost feel his sick disappointment. She wanted to cry — not for herself but for him.

'Yes, then I found you. And do you know, Emma, something happened to me at that moment. Quite suddenly, I knew that I'd been living in a world of make-believe. Deep down inside I've known for weeks that Julie wasn't in love with me; that she didn't really want to get engaged, far less to marry me. I'd known it all along only I didn't want to face up to it. And don't try to tell me I'm wrong.'

'But you are wrong, Andrew. I know she loves you. It's just that Julie's way of loving is different and . . . '

'Yes, different from the way I love and from the way you would love, isn't that right, Emma? If you were Julie, you wouldn't have carried on a flirtation with Yves Courtelle right under my nose. You wouldn't have behaved as she did, acting as if she would prefer I were somewhere else. *Would* you, Emma?'

He had stubbed out his cigarette and now he was leaning towards her, holding both her arms in a grip that hurt, though she was not conscious of it. She was aware only that this was a new Andrew; someone she didn't know; someone rough and angry and violent.

'But I'm not like Julie . . . ' she tried to explain but he wasn't really listening. He said roughly:

'No, you aren't like her. You're kind

and sweet and sensitive to a man's feelings. You're a loving kind of girl, aren't you, Emma? A giver, not a taker.'

Before she could speak, his mouth suddenly came down on hers, bruising her lips, hurting her. But she didn't mind. There was too much joy in the fact that somehow, for some strange inexplicable reason, Andrew needed her, wanted something from her; that in this moment of time, she was necessary to him as a woman.

Emma had no idea of what really went on in Andrew's mind at that moment. He was barely conscious of her as a person. He had about reached the end of his tether when he discovered that far from being Julie alone on the beach looking for her ring, it was her young sister. His reaction was almost one of hate for Emma for not being Julie; and mixed up was a hate for Julie who could treat their engagement, indeed, love itself, so lightly. He wanted to strike back at her and as she was not there, it was Emma he took in his arms and kissed so hungrily, so brutally.

Had she fought him he might still further have lost his head. But the soft response of her mouth — her whole body — brought him back to sanity. With a gradual return of his senses, he realised what was happening, what he was doing, how Emma was reacting — and he was shaken. That he, who had preached faithfulness to Julie with such fervour, could be sitting here in a car, making love to her young sister!

He released her quickly, with a hoarse apology.

'My God, Emma, I'm sorry!'

Emma bit her lip, pressing the knuckle of her hand against her mouth. She didn't fully understand what had happened but she knew one thing quite certainly — she wasn't sorry.

'Say something!' Andrew said miserably. 'Tell me I'm a brute and uncivilised and no damn good. I won't blame you.'

He sounded so hurt, she couldn't control her own swift reaction.

'Don't talk like that — I love you.'

Andrew stared at her aghast.

'Emma, no! You mustn't say that. I hope it isn't true. I'd no right to kiss you like that just now. I don't know what made me do it. Now I've húrt you, too.'

'I don't care. I don't care. I love you. I know you love Julie but even that can't stop the way I feel about you. You are the only person in the world I care about, Andrew. If it helped, kissing me, then I'm glad you did. I know it's wrong but I wanted you to. I've wanted it ever since the night you and Julie got engaged.'

The words were pouring out of her now. She couldn't stop them.

'I don't suppose you remember. It was just before your engagement was announced. You told me I looked very pretty and you kissed me — just a brotherly sort of kiss but that was the moment I first knew I loved you. I've fought against it ever since but I can't stop myself, even though I know that you are going to marry Julie.'

'But I'm not — not any more!'

His words pulled her up short as nothing else could have done. She had no ulterior motive in telling him how she felt. Her confession was entirely compulsive, without thought of consequences. She certainly had no intention of suggesting that he give up Julie and turn to her! The mere sound of his voice telling her that he wasn't going to marry Julie after all far from pleasing her, shocked her to the core.

'But, Andrew . . . you *love* her!'

'Yes, and there are times when I hate her, too. But you're right, Emma, I do love her and I always will but I'm not going to marry her. I know now she doesn't love me. No matter what you may say about her way being different from my way, what Julie feels for me isn't love. Do you know she's never once responded to my kisses the way *you* did just now? One doesn't have to be clever to feel whether a girl really wants your love or not.'

He regretted the words as soon as they were out. It wasn't fair to Emma in the first place and no matter how angry and bitter he was with Julie, he was being disloyal to her in discussing their personal relationship.

'I don't know what's got into me tonight!' he said, like a small, repentant boy. 'I apologise once more, Emma.'

Emma clasped her hands together between her knees. She was trying desperately to keep calm; to keep up with the amazing emotional turmoil Andrew was evoking. Part of her longed for him to take her in his arms again, kiss her as he had done just now. No one had ever kissed her like that. It stirred some basic response within her; a purely physical reaction of which she was afraid and at the same time, knew she wanted. She felt that she had grown up in the last ten minutes; changed for ever from a girl into a woman. And it was Andrew who had changed her.

She turned her head slowly to look at

him and a new shock awaited her, for she saw that there were tears in his eyes. The knowledge sent a wave of acute feeling right through her body and started it trembling. She had once seen a man cry on television and the sight had upset her, had made her feel vaguely uneasy all the rest of that evening. She had thought about it a lot; come to terms with the idea that men must cry sometimes just like women to relieve any great stress or sorrow. There was nothing wrong in it and yet for a man to be reduced to tears seemed to presage a grief beyond her understanding. Or an emotional stress.

Impulsively, she reached up and drew his head down as a mother might comfort her child. She felt the shuddering of his body as he fought himself and said softly:

'It's all right, Andrew. It's all right!' although she scarcely knew what her words meant. But the gentle, soothing tone of her voice seemed to get through to him, as if he guessed that she was not going to think any the less of him for breaking down.

'Oh, Julie, *Julie*!'

She heard the cry wrung from the depths of him and somehow she wasn't surprised or even hurt that it should be Julie's name he spoke with such despair. She had no thought for herself as she said quickly:

'She does love you, Andrew. I *know* she does!'

'Well, you two. Having fun?'

Aghast, Emma and Andrew drew apart at the sound of Julie's voice, harsh, strident, coming clearly through the open car window.

'Well, I must say I never thought to find this when I came out to look for my ring!' Julie was leaning in the window now, looking not at Emma but at Andrew, her eyes smiling and yet her face a mask of fury. 'Come on, now, one of you say something. 'We didn't mean to do wrong.'' Her voice was a ghastly mimicry. ''It just kind of happened!' or 'why not? We didn't mean you to find out, Julie dear!''

'Julie!' Emma's voice rang out in protest but Andrew seemed unable to speak. He sat there, staring up at Julie as if he could not believe his own eyes.

10

Emma's arms dropped to her sides at the same time that Andrew hurriedly got out of the car. Julie was already beginning to walk away from it and he hurried after her, his face white.

'Julie, stop. Come back here, Julie. Please listen to me . . . '

Emma covered her face with her hands. Her cheeks were burning and her thoughts in chaos. There was no misunderstanding Julie's bitter accusation. Perhaps she had seen Andrew kissing her! She wanted to run after Julie, explain that Andrew was still desperately in love with her; that she, Emma, had only been comforting him because he was so miserable; that there was nothing at all for Julie to mind about.

But she had to stay where she was and leave Andrew to make the explanations.

'You jumped to the wrong conclusions,

Julie,' Andrew was saying desperately to Julie's back. 'You must listen to me. Emma came out here on her own to look for the ring. Lindy found her bedroom empty and told me and it crossed my mind she might do something of the sort so I took the car and came to look for her, to give her a lift back. You know she wasn't well and . . . '

He broke off, miserably aware that there was no sign of softening in Julie's rigid body. She stood perfectly still, staring out to sea where a hazy moon was rising. She was a dark silhouette, stone-like, immovable.

'Julie, please try to understand. Emma was only doing her best to . . . to . . . '

He could not bring out the words. He was ashamed of his breakdown; unwilling to confess to Julie that his love for her had momentarily become a kind of torment and that he'd found it too much to bear alone.

Suddenly Julie swung round to face him. Her eyes were narrowed, her lips tight.

'I guessed some time ago that Emma was in love with you. And don't try to deny it, Andrew. No one who wasn't in love would turn out at this time of night to search for a damned ring that didn't even belong to them, on a deserted beach. Don't lie to me.'

Andrew's arms dropped to his sides.

'What Emma feels about me is her own affair,' he said quietly. 'And it has nothing to do with you and me, Julie. I love you. You must know that. I was angry about the ring, I admit, but it didn't stop me loving you. How could it?'

'Love!' Julie said contemptuously. 'You spend the last half hour in my sister's embrace and talk about love! Well, I'll tell you one thing, Andrew, I'm not in love with you any more. I was as upset as you about the ring — so upset I came out by myself — just like Emma . . . ' her voice was scornful . . . 'to try to find it, and what do I find instead — my fiancé making love to my sister.'

'I wasn't making love to her!'

'You didn't even kiss her then?'

Andrew felt the lie tremble on his lips. He had kissed Emma, but in a way it been Julie he was kissing; Julie he had wanted. How could he possibly make her understand.

'There you are then!' Julie cried. 'At least you're honest, Andrew, even if you are despicable in other ways. As far as I'm concerned, if you find the ring, you'd better give it to Emma next time. Maybe she'll appreciate it. I certainly don't want it back.'

She turned and began to run away from him along the beach. Andrew started to follow her and then stopped short. Coming towards them from the opposite direction was another figure — a man he did not at first recognise until he heard Julie's voice, high-pitched, calling out:

'Why, hullo, Yves!'

Abruptly, he turned on his heel and went back to the car. Emma had not moved. He got in, switched on the engine and crashing the gears, swung the car round without a word. They bumped over the sand for a moment or two before they reached the road. Then Andrew put his foot down on the accelerator and the car leapt forward.

They were almost back at the hotel before he spoke. Then in a clipped, hard voice, he said:

'The engagement's off, Emma. And don't try to put things right, because it's too late.'

Emma drew in her breath.

'Julie does love you — you said yourself that you'd have known she did if she and not I had come to look for the ring. She did come, Andrew.'

'With Yves!' Andrew said brutally. 'Oh, at first I thought as you did. I thought she was alone. But all the time, he was there. No doubt it was just an excuse to be out alone with him in the dark. Well, now she doesn't need any excuses. She can go where she wants with him when she wants.'

He drew into the parking space

outside the hotel and rammed on the brake. Then he switched off the lights and sat back, his hands still gripping the steering wheel. It was deathly quiet. Although there were lights on downstairs, no sound came to them but the slap-slap of the water against the wall of the jetty.

'I'm sorry you were involved, Emma!' he said suddenly in a quieter voice. 'I'm sorry for everything. I don't know what's going to happen now. Maybe I should go back home. I don't see how we can continue with this family holiday in these circumstances. Things won't be too good between you and Julie now, either.'

'That doesn't matter. I'll make her understand. It just can't be all over between you two. I'll talk to Julie — explain. You mustn't go home, Andrew. That way there'd be no chance of a reconciliation between you. It's all so silly — I mean, Julie must know you love her.'

Andrew's voice was bitter.

'She knows all right, but she prefers not to know. She wants to be free — free to be with the Frenchman. It was easy to see the way the wind was blowing.'

'I'll talk to her tonight,' Emma said again. 'Try not to worry, Andrew.'

Andrew leaned across her and opened the car door.

'It won't do any good. Thanks for the offer, Emma, but even if Julie did believe you, it's too late. She's told me to keep the ring if I find it . . . she doesn't want it back. And that can only mean one thing — she's in love with Yves Courtelle. So you see, I'd merely lose what shred of pride I have left if I asked her to reconsider our engagement. I don't want a fiancée who doesn't want me.'

Emma shivered. Everything looked grim and hopeless and Andrew sounded almost resigned to the worst. Somehow she herself felt guilty — as if unwittingly she had provoked this situation. If she'd minded her own business and stayed away from the beach, Julie wouldn't have found Andrew with her in the car. That at least was her fault . . .

She went up to her room, hoping that Lindy would not be waiting for her with a load of questions. What could she say to Andrew's young sister? That it was all hers, Emma's, fault?

Then Emma recalled that Yves had been with Julie — that notwithstanding the car incident, there was the question of Julie's relationship with Yves. Was Andrew right? Was Julie really attracted to the French boy? Had she after all never really loved Andrew? Despite Emma's avowal to Andrew that Julie loved him, she had often had her own doubts about it. Perhaps Andrew was nearer to the truth when he said that Julie had provoked this very situation because she wanted her freedom.

Hopelessly confused and very unhappy, Emma went to bed.

* * *

'You may wish to walk as if you were in the Olympics, but I do not!' Yves said, putting a restraining hand on Julie's arm.

Obediently she slackened her pace.

'Sorry!' she said. 'I suppose I was working off my rage or something.'

Yves sighed.

'And that, I take it, means you have had yet another quarrel with poor Andrew.'

'Poor Andrew!' Julie's voice was scornful. 'Poor Andrew was quite happily smooching in the car with my kid sister. Poor Andrew indeed!'

In the darkness, Yves smiled.

'Ah! So it is not the anger but the jealousy.'

'Jealous? Of Emma?' Julie discovered she was nearly shouting and brought her tone down an octave. 'Of course I'm not. I'm just disgusted. Andrew was the one to complain because he thought I was attracted to you — he preached faithfulness and loyalty and all that guff at me, and all the time he was encouraging my own sister. It's finished me. And as for Emma — why, she's only a child!'

'Is she, Julie? And even if you were right, and I don't agree you are, has it not occurred to you that she is a lot nicer to Andrew than you are? Personally, I wouldn't blame Andrew in the least for preferring her company to yours.'

'Yves!' Julie sounded staggered. 'What a beastly thing to say. Now you're against me, too.'

Yves laughed.

'You speak of Emma being a child, but it is you who are behaving like one now, Julie. If you will stop being angry you will admit I am right. You have not been in the least loving towards Andrew. You have been flirting with me quite openly — not even trying to disguise this from your fiancé. Can you wonder he turns to little Emma who adores him.'

'You're not seriously trying to tell me Emma's in love? Why, she's only sixteen and still at school. Andrew would never take her seriously.'

'If you believe that, Julie, why are you so concerned about them?'

'I'm not concerned!' Julie said, violently scuffing up sand with her feet as if this gave her some relief. 'I'm just disgusted with them.'

'Oh, Julie! If I did not like you so much, I would be very inclined — how do you say in English — to wash my hands of you? You want to have your cake and to eat it, too. See how well I know my English proverbs!'

'Don't say that, Yves. If you, as well as Andrew, desert me now . . . ' She broke off, suddenly miserable and unsure of herself.

'I remain your friend, Julie. That is why I tell you not to continue with such nonsense. I do not believe Andrew is in the least in love with Emma. I do not believe Emma is in love with Andrew. I think, as your fiancé, he has a certain glamour that has made little Emma *think* she loves him. After all, she is very much in your shadow, Julie. She admires you so much and wishes she were more like you. What is more natural than that she should wish also to have a handsome, attractive young man like Andrew to love and to be loved by, just as you have?'

'Emma's not in my shadow, as you put it. We've never been competitive. She's quite different from me in every way and anyway, as I said before, she's still a schoolgirl. So we've never competed for boys the way some sisters do.'

They were nearing the rocks now. Yves took Julie's arm to steady her over the rough ground.

'You do not know what goes on in Emma's mind. She has the enormous admiration for you, Julie. She thinks she can never be attractive and pretty as you are and perhaps she is right. She does not have your sparkle, your uninhibited gaiety; she is not provocative in the way you are and she knows all this. When someone falls in love with

Emma, it will be because of her serenity, her gentleness, her understanding. But she does not see these qualities as such in herself. She thinks she is plain and ordinary, which she is not.'

Julie tossed her head.

'You seem to have given young Emma quite a bit of thought! Obviously I have under-estimated her. I never once thought of her as a rival — especially over Andrew.'

The hotel was in sight now. The lights downstairs had gone out but from where they stood, they could see that in two of the upstairs bedrooms, someone was awake. 'It must be quite late,' Yves said. 'We'd better go in, Julie, but before we do, let me beg you once more to put an end to this quarrel. You do love Andrew, I think, and this is spoiling the holiday for you all. You can go to him and tell him you are sorry. I am sure he will forgive you.'

'Sorry! Forgive me!' Julie echoed. 'You don't seem to understand at all.

Yves. It's Andrew who should be sorry and I the one to forgive. If he likes to apologise to me . . . '

'Julie, you still refuse to face the truth. This is not a game you are playing where each side can tot up the score against the other. It was your initial treatment of your fiancé which provoked this situation. What followed is therefore your fault. And even that is not important. What is important is that you and Andrew should be happy together again.'

Julie wrenched her arm away from Yves' hand. Her eyes were flashing although he could not see them in the darkness.

'That's up to Andrew. I wanted to make it up. That's why I went back to the beach this evening. I thought if I could find the ring he'd realise what it meant to me, understand that I did love him. It wasn't my fault I caught him kissing Emma; nor my fault the ring was lost in the first place. He insisted I wore it. So it's up to him. He can apologise or leave things as they are. I don't much care which.'

She walked away from him, still raw with injured pride. But Yves caught her up in the doorway of the hotel.

'You said just now you wished me to remain your friend, Julie. Therefore I have to tell you that I think you are making a very big mistake — one which could bring you much unhappiness. You are behaving like a spoilt child — not as a woman, and if you are not very careful, you will lose his love.'

'If it is lost that easily,' said Julie with finality, 'then it wasn't worth having in the first place. Goodnight, Yves!'

11

By mutual agreement, none of the participants in last night's affair on the beach mentioned the broken engagement to the grown-ups; nor, of course, to the children. The ring, quite naturally, was the main topic of conversation and both sets of parents got down to the business of promoting a methodical search.

'There are ten of us altogether,' said Mr. Prescott, who prided himself on his organising ability. 'If we mark off the sand in squares of let us say three yards each, we can cover quite a large area, systematically. I will buy some sieves like Penny's and Paul's and we can sift the sand through. Then if the ring is buried we shall not miss it. In this way, one of us is bound to retrieve it.'

It was on the tip of Julie's tongue to say she had not the slightest intention of going to look for the ring again. Andrew also bit back the angry remark that he did not care whether it was found or not. Neither looked at the other nor at Emma. Only Lindy, who had wormed out of Emma the all-important fact that the engagement was off, stared from one to the other openly.

The families went down to the beach in two car loads. Yves must have had an early breakfast for he had not put in an appearance. His parents said he had gone sailing. Privately, Julie was of the belief that he was deliberately avoiding her. Andrew assumed the French boy was, guiltily, avoiding him.

For two whole hours, everyone worked under Mr. Prescott's direction, sifting their own small area of sand. The younger children began to grow bored with what had started as an exciting game. Emma felt a little sick and dizzy with bending over in the hot sun; Julie and Andrew, working as far apart as they had been able to contrive, were both feeling the effects of a sleepless night.

They were all glad when Mr. Prescott called off the search.

'I am afraid we must assume the ring has gone for good,' he said. 'I'm really very sorry indeed, Andrew!'

He, as well as his wife and Andrew's parents, imagined that the three young people's glum faces were due to the loss of the ring.

'I know it isn't quite the same, dear,' Mrs. Prescott tried to console Julie, 'but it is insured and I dare say another can be found very like it when we get back to England.'

No comment from anyone.

'Well, off you all go and have a swim,' said Mr. Prescott heartily. 'We're going to the beach hut for coffee.'

The younger children ran off happily into the water. Julie shrugged her shoulders.

'I don't feel like swimming,' she said. 'I'm going to walk into Benodet and do some shopping.'

Emma waited for Andrew to offer to go with her, drive her there if needs be, but he merely turned away from Julie. To Emma and his sister, he said:

'What about some crabbing? The tide's just gone out and we may find some good ones.'

Lindy was enthusiastic. Too old to build sandcastles, crabbing was still permissible enjoyment in her view, and she ran off ahead of Andrew and Emma, brandishing her fishing net and one of the children's plastic buckets.

Emma took the opportunity to say to Andrew:

'I haven't been able to talk to Julie yet. I did get her by herself on the stairs before breakfast but when I tried to say anything, she shut me up. It's almost as if she doesn't want me to explain.'

Andrew sighed.

'I told you last night I don't think she does want to put things right. Forget it, Emma. If that's all I mean to her, it's better I should find out now. I'm honestly beginning to think I don't much care anyway.'

But both knew he was lying. He was

desperately worried and unhappy but he could think of no way of putting things right. He was also sick with jealousy. He had waited up to watch for Julie's return last night; seen her walking arm in arm with Yves over the rocks; seen them pause, talking together in a way he had taken to be very intimate. He had little doubt now that Julie was involved with Yves. The way the French boy had made himself scarce this morning only confirmed his view. Yves couldn't face him.

For all he knew, Julie had a private arrangement to meet Yves in Benodet this morning. But for her behaviour with the French boy, he might well have followed her, tried to make her understand that she had no cause to be jealous of poor little Emma.

He looked down at the girl beside him, partly with feelings of guilt, partly with affection. At least *she* cared that he was unhappy; was willing to do what she could to put things right. In view of what she had said last night about being in love with him — not that he'd taken it very seriously — she was behaving in a very selfless way. One day some man was going to fall in love with little Emma and think himself a lucky chap. And that day wasn't so far off. She might be only sixteen but she was mature for her age; much more mature than he had realised. He found himself wondering if last night was the first time anyone had kissed Emma. He'd felt badly about it, too. Her first kiss ought to have come from someone who really cared about her.

'Not that I don't,' Andrew told himself truthfully. 'I care a great deal and it's a damned shame she has to be hurt by Julie and me!'

He linked his arm in hers affectionately.

'You're a sweet kid, Emma!' he said. 'I hope you've forgiven me for last night.'

Emma felt a rush of conflicting emotions. Andrew's touch, his words, sent the colour surging to her cheeks.

They made her happy and at the same time, miserable, for his tone of voice was, somehow, brotherly. He was treating her as a schoolgirl again, not, as he had done last night, as a woman.

She found herself gently removing her arm from his on the pretext of bending down to look at a brightly coloured sea-anemone in one of the rock pools. Then Lindy came rushing over to them to see what Emma had found and there was no further discussion between them. Emma was glad of Lindy's presence. She was no longer at ease alone in Andrew's company.

Julie managed to create a further disturbance by not returning to the beach before lunch. Instead, she caught a bus to the village and walked back to the hotel. The rest of the family — Andrew in particular nervous and anxious — awaited her return until after one o'clock and then decided to leave without her. When they found her already at the hotel, Andrew, relieved, vented his anxiety in a burst of anger.

'You might at least have told us you were finding your own way home,' he stormed at her. 'I suppose it never occurred to you you'd keep us all hanging around, worried stiff!'

Julie looked at him coolly, eyebrows raised.

'Worried? Whatever about? I should have thought you'd all realise I wouldn't walk back along that beach road when I could perfectly well get a bus. It seemed to me to be the *logical* thing to do.'

Andrew was about to argue the point but she turned away and went into the dining room ahead of him. Yves was already at the table. Julie went straight over to him and enquired about his morning's sailing.

'Sounds marvellous!' she said in a high, false voice. 'Are you going again this afternoon? If so, do take me with you. I've had enough of the beach.'

Yves looked past her to Andrew, now sitting down opposite him.

'What about it, Andrew?' he asked pleasantly. To Julie's annoyance he included Andrew in the plan. 'It really was very enjoyable this morning. I think you would like it.'

Andrew threw him a look of disgust. It seemed to him as if the French boy were deliberately taunting him.

'No, thanks!' he said shortly. 'I've other plans.'

'Then we'll go on our own!' Julie said, smiling a little too obviously at Yves. 'It'll be fun!'

'What about you, Emma?' Yves was still not giving in. He wouldn't in the least mind going alone with Julie but he had no intention of letting her use him as a weapon with which to hurt Andrew.

Emma hesitated. She didn't want to go but at the same time, she felt that Andrew did not want Julie to go alone with Yves.

Julie said:

'Emma doesn't know how to sail,' and she sat down and poured herself a glass of the local wine they now drank at meal times. 'Do you, Emma?' she added too brightly.

'Then is it not time she learned?' Yves put in before Emma could reply.

Andrew did not understand Yves. He had expected him to jump at the chance of taking Julie out alone. Now he seemed determined to drag Emma along as a chaperone.

He decided that Yves was merely attempting to allay his suspicions. Not that it could make much difference, one way or the other, how he felt. He wasn't engaged to Julie any more and if she chose, she could go out with Yves or anyone else she wanted.

'But, Emma,' Lindy was saying. 'You promised you'd come fishing with me this afternoon on the beach. Mother is taking the others on a picnic and I hate picnics.'

Emma sighed. It was perfectly true that she had promised to go off with Lindy.

'That's settled then,' said Julie, with a

triumphant look at Andrew. 'Yves and I will go on our own.'

'I have not yet made up my mind to go,' said Yves, but he could think of no valid reason to refuse.

Later, as he guided the small craft out to sea, he looked at Julie's set, determined little face and said:

'You really wish to burn your fingers, do you not, Julie? Or is it that you wish to hurt Andrew because you think he has hurt you?'

Julie glanced up at the jib and hauled it in a fraction.

'I don't know what you're talking about, Yves. I just wanted to come sailing. I love it. It's as simple as that.'

He leant down and wedged the baler more securely into the locker. The boat heeled slightly at a small gust of wind and automatically Yves slackened the sheet. They were once more on an even keel.

'The wind is not so steady as it was this morning,' Yves commented. He looked up at the sky speculatively.

'Sometimes these slight gusts mean a stronger wind is coming. Maybe after all, we should not try to go to the island.'

'Oh, but I want to!' cried Julie. Yves had told her during their last sailing expedition about the little ruined chapel on the island six miles off the coast. No one lived there now although it had been occupied long ago and the Germans had built fortifications there in the last war.

'We can reach the island easily enough,' Yves said thoughtfully. 'But coming back, we must beat against the wind. If it gets up this could be difficult and very uncomfortable.'

'You're not afraid, are you, Yves? I thought you considered yourself an expert helmsman?'

Although he half realised that it was both stupid and dangerous to be affected in one's decisions by a 'dare', Yves could not resist that challenge. He reddened.

'I am not afraid for myself, Julie. But

I am responsible for you,' he said angrily.

'And I am responsible for myself!' Julie retorted. 'I want to go on — please, Yves!'

Yves hesitated. There were no further gusts of wind and the blue sea around them looked calm and unmenacing. He thrust aside the vague misgivings of a moment ago. He, himself, wished to see the island which he had only once visited before. It was possible to find the most beautiful sea-shells there. He knew they would fascinate Julie; and they might also see some rare butterflies of great size and beauty. The chapel ruins were definitely worth a visit; glorious old stone, covered now in wild flowers and creepers. Sea birds would be nesting on the rocks. He argued no more.

Having got her own way, Julie sat back contentedly. There was little for her to do as Yves nursed the boat along. Once or twice they passed other small craft whose occupants waved gaily to them and called out a greeting. But soon they were away from the coast and the outline of the island came more clearly into perspective. Julie was able to make out the fascinating shape of the chapel tower.

She leaned over suddenly to call Yves' attention to this and at that moment, a sharp flurry of wind hit them broadside. The boat heeled violently and a small wave slapped in, drenching Julie's white jeans.

Instinctively Yves strained his body's weight outwards to balance the small craft. The boat righted itself to his reaction but now there was no doubt that the wind was freshening in an alarming way.

Soon they were less than a mile from the island and assessing the weather and the distances involved, Yves made the decision to go on rather than turn for home. He had little time to think further, for he had to fight the boat which was kicking violently now, with a life and will of its own.

Julie, aware of the crisis, sat perfectly

still. There was little she could do to help until Yves issued a command. She glanced up and saw the sky was darkening ominously with angry clouds. The sea around them was no longer blue but a sullen, white-flecked grey. Small foam-crested waves rose sharply and slapped the side of the boat with threatening regularity.

It was with a sense of relief that Julie saw the tiny harbour in front of them. The jetty had long since crumbled but inside the small breakwater, the sea was calm enough to offer comparatively safe anchorage.

Yves' face had become a mask of concentration. He knew that the next few moments were going to be difficult. It was going to require split-second judgement to decide the exact moment to spill the wind from the sails. To leave this too late would mean an inevitable smash up on the rocks.

He let out a sigh of relief as the small boat answered his command and swung round to a stop, canvas slapping noisily but idly now, around their heads. The first few icy drops of rain began to fall as he and Julie lowered the sails and lashed them against the boom. Then without a word Yves loosened one of the light oars and paddled towards the jetty.

Julie jumped out first and caught the rope he threw to her. She stood there holding it until he joined her and tied it to a mooring firmly cemented to the side of the jetty.

'I hope she won't bump herself to pieces against these stones,' Yves said, looking anxiously at the boat. 'But there is little I can do to prevent it.'

The rain came lashing down, soaking them both to the skin. It muffled the clang of a bell on the rocks above them. Head lowered against the wind, wordlessly Yves took Julie's arm. Together they ran towards the chapel.

12

Andrew was furiously angry. Julie had publicly humiliated him and he would never forgive her. As far as he was concerned, she could go off with Yves Courtelle and never come back. It really was the end of everything between them.

'Perhaps,' he thought bitterly, 'that was exactly what Julie had in mind when she threw herself at Yves' head at lunch time.' Her manner had been so blatant that even Yves had looked embarrassed. Otherwise, why should he try to cover up their intrigue by inviting Emma to join their little tête-à-tête?

Andrew drove his car recklessly along the narrow road that led away from the hotel. He had to get away from them all — far away. In fact, it was at the back of his mind to go home to England but this would involve him in explanations to the two families, which he couldn't yet face. It was all he could do to face the situation alone. He kept having to remind himself that he and Julie were all washed up. Their engagement was off.

He had another reason for not going back home. He wasn't going to let Julie see how hurt he was. He had a little pride left. He'd stay on and find some way of showing Julie that he could have as good a time — better even — without her.

He came out onto the main road to Benodet and his thoughts turned to Emma. He was very fond of Julie's young sister. The previous night had been a revelation to him — he'd simply never thought of her as grown up before. He supposed he'd always been subconsciously aware of her devotion to him but had accepted it without analysis. The discovery that she thought herself in love with him complicated that past easy friendship. He was ashamed of the way he had behaved to

212

her. He was not by nature selfish and yet he knew he had 'used' her as a substitute for Julie; someone on whom he could expend the excess emotion Julie had roused in him. At the time, of course, it had just happened. Without stopping to think about it, he had kissed little Emma. And he should have stopped to think. At Emma's age, kissing wasn't something, anything to be taken lightheartedly as Julie did — or at least, as she had seemed to take it. He had asked himself over and over again if she had ever kissed Yves. He was sure that she had. He had no reason, therefore, to feel guilty about having embraced Emma — at least, not on Julie's account. But he did feel guilty about Emma. He was fond of her. He respected her, but nothing more positive.

Andrew pulled his thoughts up with a jerk. He had been so lost in them, he'd stopped concentrating on his driving. He found himself on the left side of the road. Shaken, he pulled sharply back onto the right and brought the car to a stop. If that was the best way he could drive abroad, then he'd better go home tomorrow. He wasn't so miserable that he wanted to commit suicide!

He lit a cigarette and tried to relax, but already his mind was once more reliving the events of the past twenty-four hours. The memory of Julie's face, laughing up at Yves, challenging him to take her sailing, caught at his heart. She was so lovely — and so cruel. What a fool he'd been ever to imagine she loved him.

He glanced out of the window and saw that the sun had gone in. Small dark clouds were beginning to gather in the sky over to the west. For a moment Andrew watched them moving in his direction. He frowned. There was little doubt the weather was deteriorating. He knew that it could change rapidly on this part of the coast. He wondered if Yves had checked the weather forecast before he set off. He was aware that they had gone off to the island

— Emma had told him before she went out with Lindy. Kind little Emma! With her strange sensitivity, she'd known he was aching to find out where Yves and Julie were going. Not that the knowledge made him any happier. He at once told himself Yves had especially chosen the island so that they could disembark and have the afternoon unencumbered by sailing, alone together.

Vindictively he was glad the weather was changing. If the wind got up, Yves would have to bring Julie back. Then he tried to squash the spiteful thought. What he really wanted was not to care what was happening to them. He wanted to feel as indifferent to Julie as he did to Emma.

But was he, after all, so indifferent to little Emma? Not entirely. Her devotion to him was the one shred of comfort to his shattered heart. At least *she* found something about him to love. She didn't think, like Julie, that he was dull, a bore. She had taken his side over the ring, too. If Julie had really valued it, she'd never have allowed it to get lost.

'For two pins,' Andrew told himself, 'I'd take Emma out tonight — to a cinema or something.'

Julie wouldn't like that. She'd been jealous enough when she'd found Emma in the car with him — imagining a set-up that had never existed. Maybe it would serve her right, prove to her just how little he cared about Julie, if he took her young sister out again.

But he knew he would not do this. It wasn't fair to Emma. He must take care not to make use of her. She loved him and although he couldn't return that love at least he could take care of her; guard her from himself.

He almost smiled at the idea of having to guard anyone from himself. But it wasn't really so impossible. He had found a moment of comfort in the car with Emma — she'd been gentle and tender and entirely sympathetic. It would be all too easy to give way to the temptation to let her comfort him as best she could.

Andrew switched on the engine but did not at once restart the car. The sky had darkened even more whilst he had sat brooding and now rain splashed at intervals against the windscreen. Maybe he should drive back to the hotel. He'd not been going anywhere special — merely felt the need to drive off somewhere alone. But if there was to be a storm, someone in the family party might need help. The two sets of parents and the young children would be all right, for they had one car into which they could all pile for the drive home. But Emma and Lindy were out on the rocks. Not that he could reach them by car but he was sure, for instance, that they wouldn't have thought of taking their macs. They'd appreciate these.

Andrew turned the car round and began to drive back to the hotel. He was well aware of the fact that his idea of offering assistance to Emma and Lindy was only a feeble excuse for his return. The two girls could easily scramble back across the rocks alone and it wouldn't hurt them to get wet. No, his real reason was his growing concern for Julie and Yves. He could feel the gusts of wind against the car wheels; knew that sailing would not be easy in these conditions; knew that the conditions were rapidly getting worse.

★　★　★

They were out of breath when they reached the chapel ruins. The clanging of the bell vied with the noise of the wind so that they had to raise their voices and shout at each other.

'No shelter here — the roof's non-existent!' Julie cried.

Yves stared round anxiously. The four walls stood partly erect but, as Julie had said, the roof had long since fallen in and the floor of the chapel was a mass of rubble and loose stones, and tall coarse grass. Only the little belfry still lifted its head bravely up to the sky, supporting the rusty old bell that was swinging violently to and fro in the wild wind.

'You stay here!' he told Julie, and pushed her up against the tower where there was at least shelter from the wind if not from the rain. 'I'll go and see if there's anywhere better. There's going to be one bad hell of a storm!'

He disappeared without waiting for her to reply.

Julie relaxed against the rough wall and gradually got back her breath. She felt a stinging pain in one knee and bent down to find she had somehow gashed it, tearing her jeans and exposing the grazed skin beneath. She found a handkerchief in her anorak pocket and dabbed at the blood.

She wasn't really frightened. The storm excited her as much as their dash across the rocks to the chapel to beat the rain which was now beginning to fall more heavily. But she felt nervy and shivered — feeling the cold raindrops against her face and the wind playing havoc with her hair. The bell went on clanging above her head with a deafening noise.

She saw herself as she might see the heroine in a film and the idea appealed to her. This was real-life adventure and she, Julie Prescott, was in the middle of it. She had been able to guess from the set concentration on Yves' face that they had been momentarily in danger when he'd brought in the boat. Now that the danger was past she could enjoy it in retrospect. She imagined telling the rest of the family when they got back. Emma would wish she had come after all.

Emma! The expression on Julie's face changed. She still found it difficult to believe that Emma was grown up — a kind of rival. Seeing Andrew in the car with her had been a nasty shock. She hadn't really believed Andrew had been kissing her sister and her accusation had been meant more as a question than a statement of fact. But their faces — as much as the fact that Andrew still had his arms round Emma — had warned her that it wasn't merely her imagination playing tricks.

She tried to analyse the emotions that had torn through her at the time. She'd felt physically sick . . . and yet behind it all, lay incredulity. Emma . . . and Andrew! It still didn't seem possible. But for Yves, she might not have taken it so much to heart; even discredited it despite the evidence of her own eyes. But Yves had warned her. Emma might not be as pretty as Julie but she had something else — some special appeal of her own. Beside which, Emma had, so Yves said, been so much nicer to Andrew than she, Julie.

'Well, she can have him!' Julie thought viciously. 'To think that my own sister has been trying to take my boy friend from me behind my back! I was too stupid to see it.

But no matter what, she still couldn't bring herself to see Emma, her kid sister, as a seductress. It was too absurd. Em wasn't long out of a gym tunic! Yet if she had grown up suddenly, maybe Andrew as well as Yves saw what she, Julie, had not seen — that Emma was now very attractive. Yves thought so — so why not Andrew?

'If he is interested in her, it's only on the rebound!' Julie told herself. 'He came after me after the car episode.'

Suddenly feeling cold and depressed, she wondered if she should have waited on the beach to hear Andrew's explanation. But she did not linger on that thought. She was finished with Andrew. Yves was a much more interesting companion. She liked the way he told her off when she was behaving badly! She liked his ability to resist her. Andrew always gave in so easily. She sensed that Yves was half way to being in love with her and she felt the challenge — wanted to make him fall completely — the way Andrew had.

Yves seemed to have been gone a long time. She looked anxiously at the arched entrance, still intact, watching for his return. Her relief when at last he came towards her, made her laugh.

'You look half-drowned!' she told him.

'And so I am!' Yves acknowledged, shaking himself like a dog to get the rainwater off his hair and anorak. 'Come on, Mademoiselle Julie. I have found somewhere for us to take shelter. It isn't quite like your Buckingham Palace, but at least it will keep us dry.'

He took her arm and hurried her out of the chapel and further into the island. The ground was rocky and slippery and they stumbled forward, the rain driving into their faces. They seemed to be climbing slightly. Julie felt the pull on her leg muscles but Yves dragged her on and would not let her stop to rest. The noise of the bell grew less and soon was muffled by the wind. Once, they disturbed a gull. The strong-winged bird flew into the air screaming furiously.

Julie was all but staggering with exhaustion when at last Yves pulled her after him through an opening of some kind and they both fell forward in a heap onto the floor.

For a moment they lay gasping. Then Julie sat up, aware that there was a strange quiet after the tempest outside, and that it was dark. Also, the floor on which she sat was dry.

'It's an old German gun emplacement,' Yves said. 'We cannot see out through those slits in the walls because of the rain but I've little doubt from here there would be a fine view out to sea.'

'First time I've ever felt grateful to the Germans for their war effort!' Julie laughed. 'It's beautifully dry in here.'

'And we are not so beautifully wet!' said Yves. 'Take off your anorak, Julie, and your shoes and socks. Here, I will help you!'

When she had peeled off her wet socks, Julie suddenly realised how cold her feet were. Until then, she had scarcely noticed this. Yves took each in turn on his lap and rubbed until the circulation came back. Then he massaged her hands.

Soon she was glowing with warmth, cheeks pink, eyes bright, lips smiling at him gratefully.

'Better?' he asked, returning her smile.

'Wonderful!' Julie said. Impulsively she leant forward and kissed him. 'There, that's for being so nice,' she said. 'You are — what do you say? — *bien gentil!*'

Yves took out a handkerchief and passed it to Julie, indicating that she might use it to dry her hair. It hung in wet strands across her face but even then she looked extremely pretty and attractive and very feminine.

'*Bien gentil* is good French. *Nice* is a funny English word. I think perhaps stupid is a better description of me. We should not . . . and I mean *not* . . . have come sailing this afternoon. I let you talk me into it, Julie, against my better judgement. And what is more, I do not take notice of the weather. Now it is possible this storm could continue for some time and we shall not be able to get back.'

Julie looked up at him quickly from beneath a veil of hair she was rubbing dry with the handkerchief. She grimaced at him. 'You mean we might be stuck here all night?'

Yves' face grew serious

'Yes. Sometimes these storms continue for a long time. We have no food, no water and worst of all, no matches with which to lit a fire. It will be most unpleasant.'

To his surprise Julie laughed.

'*I* think it will be fun. One thing we won't be short of is water,' she indicated the rain teeming down outside. 'We may be hungry but I don't see why we should be cold. It's as snug as anything in here.'

Slowly Yves' face relaxed.

'You are always surprising me, Julie. I make up my mind that you are a spoilt little girl and then you accept this very unhappy predicament in which we find ourselves with great good humour.'

Julie laughed again.

'Oh, that's the Girl Guide in me

— I've always enjoyed camping. Anyway, I don't see it's so terrible. I mean, we do have shelter and we have each other for company. I think it's rather fun.'

'Fun?' Yves shrugged his shoulders. 'This is a word like '*nice*' you use very often. It is important to you, this having fun?'

Julie giggled.

'Well, I suppose so, yes! I don't want to get old and staid and dull just yet. I want to have lots and lots of fun — stay young for ages and ages.' She shook her hair out of her eyes and leant back on her hands. 'Maybe that's why I'm not all that keen on marrying Andrew. I'm not really ready to settle down and be a housewife. Can't you understand that, Yves?'

He thought for a moment then said:

'I do not myself see why marriage should be dull. Most certainly not if one is married to the right person. It would seem to me that you could have a great deal of 'fun' if there were two of you to enjoy everything together.'

Julie raised her eyebrows.

'I never thought of it that way,' she admitted. 'I just thought of marriage the way it is for my parents. They never go out much — just sit and watch television night after night. Dad goes to the local occasionally and Mum has the odd day in London shopping. But most of the time she is busy looking after all of us and I'd hate to live like that.'

'Did Andrew want you to have a family at once?'

'Good gracious, no!' Julie sounded surprised. 'Far from it. He said he wanted me to himself for years and years before he had to share me with anyone else.'

'Then you would not have been tied as your Maman is to domesticity,' pointed out Yves.

Julie nodded.

'No, I suppose not. But I would be tied in another way, wouldn't I? Just look how annoyed Andrew was with me because you and I became friends.'

Yves held out his hands in a gesture

that was typically French.

'Julie, you know as well as I do that Andrew had every right to be annoyed — or at least, uneasy. You are very attractive and I am a young unattached man. What else could you expect from your future husband?'

'He might have trusted me!' Julie replied and then grinned mischievously at Yves. 'Not that I'm saying I am to be trusted. Anyway, I'm free now. My engagement is well and truly off so if you feel like kissing me, no one can object.'

For a moment Yves grinned back at her, then his face became suddenly serious.

'I shall not kiss you, Julie — not because I don't wish to do so but because I think you only suggested it to see how I would react. And I'm certainly not going to be one of your little experiments.'

Julie rolled over on her side and looked up under her lashes, her enormous blue eyes fixed on the French boy.

'You're not going to be an old goody-goody like Andrew?'

'*Goody-goody*? These English words! If it means what I think, then that is exactly how I intend to behave. We may be here all night, Julie. If I were to start kissing you, we might not find it so easy to stop.'

'That might be fun, too!' Julie's voice was less sure of itself. She wasn't in love with Yves and they both knew it. A flirtation was one thing but she really didn't want anything more.

Suddenly Yves put a hand beneath her chin and tilted her face upwards so that she was forced to look directly into his eyes.

'Yesterday you tried to make me believe that you were far from a — how do you say — goody-goody?' His accent made her smile briefly. 'But I do not think this is so, is it? You have never been with a man, have you, Julie? Not even with Andrew.'

Julie was fiery red now but tossed her head, reluctant to relinquish her woman-of-the-world image.

'I don't see why I should answer that,' she prevaricated.

'Don't you?' Yves' voice was suddenly different, almost angry — certainly forceful. 'Then I will tell you. If I knew that I was not to be the first — that you made a habit of this, then you would not be lying there trying to tempt me. No, Julie, I would be trying to tempt you. I am, after all, a man like any other. Or perhaps not like many others. It is perhaps fortunate that I see behind the image of yourself you chose to give me. I see that I have to take care of you, Julie, but there are others who in these circumstances would not.'

Julie twisted out of his grasp, pouting.

'You're just as bad as Andrew. I can take care of myself. I'm not entirely helpless.'

Yves drew a deep breath. Already once he had tried to teach her a lesson; make her understand that playing with a man's emotions was like playing with fire. No man could stay so close to her and not be stirred to desire. He had little doubt that if he once started making love to her, Julie would not want to stop at just a kiss or two. Or even if she wished it, he could soon make her feel otherwise, physically. The mere fact that she did not realise this, only increased his certainty that she knew very little about life — or men.

He stood up and walked across to one of the slit windows, staring out into the rain. He felt suddenly quite old. It had a grim humour — this bizarre situation in which he found himself. Here he was, alone on an uninhabited island miles from anywhere or anyone with a girl who was all but asking to be seduced and yet he would not do so. He must be more of an idealist than he had supposed — or more chivalrous.

Julie lay where she was, staring at Yves' back with a puzzled frown. She really did not understand men. She knew Yves found her attractive. A girl always knew. She'd told him she'd like to be kissed and he was rejecting the offer — for her own good.

'What's *wrong* with me?' she said aloud.

Yves turned and looked at her, a half smile playing at the corners of his mouth.

'There is nothing *wrong* with you, Julie. It is only your thinking which is muddled. Sex is not something you should separate from love. If you are to find happiness, then the two must go hand in hand. You have become a little bored with Andrew because you know with him you are sexually quite safe. You know he has far too much respect for you to try to make love to you before you are married. So you turned to me. But it is not me you really want, Julie. There is nothing wrong that marriage to Andrew would not put right.'

'Marriage to *Andrew*!' Julie echoed. 'What a silly thing to say when I'm not even engaged to him any more.'

Yves laughed outright at her furious face.

'Personally, I think engagements are very unsatisfactory arrangements. One is neither one thing nor the other. When I find a girl I wish to marry, I shall not become engaged but marry her at once.'

He went over and sat down beside her. Julie had relaxed and suddenly there was no tension between them.

'It's funny, really,' Julie mused. 'No one's ever talked to me the way you have, Yves. You are often almost rude and you say just what you think whether you believe I'll like to hear it or not. I can be honest with you because you are with me. It's like having a very special elder brother, only better!'

Yves laughed. 'I would find it very difficult to think of you as my sister, Julie. You are far too pretty!'

Julie sniffed.

'You say that, yet you couldn't contemplate falling in love with me. Could you?'

Yves laughed again.

'I might. But we should not suit each

other, Julie. You may not know it, but I, too, have a very quick temper, and like you, I am rather spoilt. I think the girl I marry must be quiet and gentle and full of understanding. Like Emma, I think.'

'Emma!' Julie felt like bursting into tears. 'So you find my kid sister more attractive?'

'I did not say that. I do not think she can compare with you, Julie. You are what we French call the *coquette*. This has much appeal to a man. But so also has Emma. There is something very sweetly feminine about her — a serenity that is to my liking.'

'And obviously to Andrew's, too!'

Yves' eyebrows were raised meaningfully.

'Then you are jealous, Julie, and this means that you do still have some feelings for Andrew.'

'No, it doesn't. I just can't get used to the idea of Emma — *Emma* as a kind of *femme fatale* — in opposition to me!'

'That she is most certainly not — but

one day . . . ' Yves left the sentence unfinished.

'Oh, bother Emma!' Julie cried. 'And please do kiss me, Yves. I promise — honestly — to be good!'

13

Andrew drew Emma to one side and said:

'You're quite sure they were going to the island, Em? I don't want to worry your parents if there is nothing to worry about. If they went somewhere along the coast, they could put in when it got rough. But if they went to the island . . . '

Emma looked up at him helplessly.

'Julie *said* the island. You don't think they'll capsize or anything?'

'God only knows!' Andrew retorted. 'And frankly, I'm almost past caring. It's typical of Julie to get herself and everyone else into danger by sheer thoughtlessness. I warned them last time they went sailing that it was too rough and look what happened.'

Emma bit her lip.

'Andrew, you can't blame Julie. The

weather was perfectly all right when they set out. And Yves is supposed to be an expert sailor. I'm sure he wouldn't have taken her if he'd thought there was any danger.'

'Probably not, he's so devoted to her!' Andrew said childishly. 'I wonder if there's a life boat or something similar for cases like this, and if so, whether we ought to call them out.'

'Then you *do* think they are in trouble?'

Andrew glanced out of the hotel window. The rain was now lashing down and the *femme de chambre* had had to close all the bedroom shutters to prevent them crashing against the glass in the strong wind.

'They must be. It's to be hoped they reached the island before the storm broke. But if they did, they'll be stuck there all night. There isn't a chance of getting back in this.'

'Perhaps I'd better tell Mother,' Emma suggested.

'No, don't!' Andrew broke in. 'It'll

only worry her and there's nothing much your parents can do that I can't do anyway. I'll go down to the jetty and find out from one of the fishermen what the score is.'

'I'll come with you,' Emma said at once. 'I'd like to, Andrew, please. I'm as worried as you are.'

Andrew hesitated for a moment and then nodded. They'd both get soaked through but if Emma didn't mind . . .

The jetty was deserted except for the ferry driver who was making his little motor launch more secure. He had on seamen's yellow oilskins and was better protected than Andrew or Emma who wore only their anoraks.

Andrew had some difficulty in making himself understood.

'Two people — sailing — to island!' he said for about the fourth time before the man understood. Andrew pointed vaguely in the direction Yves and Julie had gone. 'Bad weather. Capsize. Is there a boat with engine — life boat? Who can go and look for them?'

The man rattled off a reply in Breton which neither Emma nor Andrew could possibly understand.

'Boat — like this? *Comme ça?*' Andrew shouted against the wind, pointing to the launch.

The man frowned, shrugging his shoulders. It seemed he had at least understood that they wanted a boat like his. He shook his head.

'*Non, non!*' he said violently. He pointed to the sea and made swift up and down movements with his hand.

'He's trying to tell us it's too rough,' Andrew said. He made another attempt.

'Not far — *pas loin*. Eight kilometers. *Huit kilometres!*'

He put his hand in his pocket and drew out his wallet. The men watched him silently and then once again shook his head. Then without another word, he turned on his heel and left them.

'*Is* it too rough for that boat?' Emma asked, 'or is he just unwilling to go out in the storm?'

'I think the boat would be safe

enough,' Andrew said. 'After all, it's a fairly substantial one and the sea's not all that rough for a boat this size.'

'But he won't let us take it, will he?'

She watched Andrew's face and understanding made her gasp:

'You're not going to take it without his permission?'

Andrew grinned.

'Why not? He obviously doesn't intend to run the ferry in this gale and anyway, no one's going to want to cross over while it's teeming. We'll be back before he needs it again, and even if we're not, we can pretend we misunderstood him.'

Emma's eyes danced with excitement. Andrew might not have realised it, but he had said 'we'. That meant he was going to take her, too.

'I suppose you ought not to come along,' Andrew said as if he had read her thoughts. 'But I may need you to bale if we ship a lot of water. Jump in, then, Emma. We'll try it out. Quickly, before someone see us and tries to prevent us going.'

He helped her down the steps and into the boat. For a moment, he wondered whether the ferryman might hear the engine start but the wind muffled the noise as he started it up. He settled himself comfortably at the tiller and they moved away from the jetty. Within minutes, the heavy rain had obscured them from the view of anyone on land. Andrew relaxed.

'Our biggest headache is finding the island!' he said. 'I had a good look at the map before we came out and it's only marked with a dot. I've got the general direction and distance but with this visibility, we aren't going to see it unless we run right into it. I'm really banking on the rain letting up before we get there — give us a chance to see it, then.'

He looked at Emma's face, shining with rain, her hair already dripping as if she had washed it.

'You look half drowned, Em!' he shouted.

'So do you!'

He laughed. For the first time in days, he almost felt happy. He guessed Julie would be feeling pretty silly by now, marooned on the island. Yves, too, was going to lose face. For an experienced sailor, he ought to know better. They could thank their lucky stars they had him, Andrew, to rescue them. For once, Julie might realise just what he could do when he wanted.

He looked down at the water slapping against the side of the boat and saw that the tide was running with them. He suddenly wondered how much petrol there was in the tank. There was no way of telling. Then he saw a can beside Emma's feet and relaxed. Obviously the chap carried a spare gallon or two on board. With only eight kilometres to go there and back, they'd be all right. There'd be enough to stooge around for a while, too, if they couldn't find the island immediately.

Emma moved over cautiously and sat beside him so that they need not shout at one another.

'Lucky we were both still dressed for out of doors,' she said. 'If we'd had to go back for anoraks, someone would have been sure to ask what we were up to.'

'It'll get rougher in a minute,' Andrew cautioned. 'It's bound to once we get out of the estuary. So sit tight, Emma. I can't jump into the sea and rescue you *and* mind the boat!'

Andrew was right. The waves were considerably higher as they reached the open sea. Every few minutes one of them spilled itself into the boat. Emma got busy bailing. Andrew was having to use all his strength now to hang on to the tiller.

It did not occur to Emma to feel frightened. She had complete faith in Andrew and in his ability to go wherever he wanted. She took it for granted they'd find the island, rescue Yves and Julie and reach home safely. But Andrew did not have the same unconcern. It was rougher than he had expected and the boat was sluggish and heavy to handle. He was beginning to see why the ferryman had shaken his head.

His common sense told him to turn for home. But the thought of Julie alone on the island with the French boy, prevented him from taking the sensible view. He couldn't even be sure they were safe on the island. Their boat might have overturned and the two of them be clinging to it, calling desperately and hopelessly for help.

The thought of Julie in real danger made him feel physically sick. He knew he'd never be able to go back to the hotel and just wait for them to turn up when the storm abated. He couldn't — no matter how dangerous this rescue attempt. If only he hadn't brought Emma with him. He'd no right to endanger her life, too.

She looked up from her task and met his stare uncomprehendingly. He realised that she had no awareness of the danger and that her confidence in him was total. It both demoralised him and stiffened his intention. He'd show everyone that he could do something worth while; that he wasn't the inadequate fool Julie no doubt thought him after his emotional breakdown in the car. The memory was highly embarrassing to him. Strangely not with Emma who seemed if not to understand, at least not to think it strange that a grown man should cry. It was as if she understood the strain he'd been under since they'd come out here; the strain of loving Julie hopelessly and desperately and knowing she didn't love or need him.

Well, she needed him now.

Andrew pulled his thoughts back to the job in hand. The rain did seem to have slackened a bit although the wind, if anything, was stronger. They must have better visibility if they were to find the island. The thought of that tiny black dot on the map was unnerving. It was so small and this grey-green ocean all around them so vast!

A glance at his watch told him it was

four o'clock. At least they didn't have to worry about nightfall. With luck, they should all be safely back in the hotel by dark.

'I think it's stopped raining!' Emma shouted as she tipped another load of water back into the sea. Her arm and back were aching but she didn't really feel it.

Andrew nodded.

'Reckon we've done at least five kilometres. Visibility's better. If we're going in the right direction, we ought to be able to see the island fairly soon.'

The 'if' was a much bigger supposition than Emma could guess. He was steering with nothing but the minute compass set in the strap of his watch. He knew only that they were travelling in a south-easterly direction.

Emma saw the island first. When she pointed excitedly behind him, he could see only a faint blur against the horizon, but five minutes later he was sure Emma was right. There was land of some kind out there. Unless they had travelled in a circle and hit the coast further round, then it had to be the island. He felt a great wave of thankfulness sweep over him.

'We'll make it for sure now!' he shouted triumphantly.

It was at that moment that the engine, working smoothly and easily until then, suddenly coughed, stopped, began again and then with a last splutter, died.

'Damn and blast!' Andrew muttered under his breath. 'Out of fuel. Pass that can over, Em.'

Emma bent down to lift the can. The moment she did so she knew something was wrong; knew that it was serious. The can was far too light. It must be empty.

'Hurry it up!' Andrew called impatiently. Then he saw Emma's face. 'Oh, no!' he cried. 'Don't tell me . . . it's not empty?'

Unable to say the words he didn't want to hear, Emma could only nod.

'That's torn it,' said Andrew. 'Now

we really are in a mess!'

For a moment, he stared from Emma's white anxious face to the empty can in her hand and back again. He was not yet willing to face up to his own stupidity in not checking on the can's contents before leaving. He had no justification for assuming it was full. It was perhaps the most elementary of all precautions before you took a boat to sea — to make sure there was adequate fuel — and oars . . .

He glanced quickly round the boat and breathed a long sigh of relief. There were oars neatly stowed along the locker on the port side.

'It's not quite so desperate, after all!' he told Emma as reassuringly as he could. 'We've got oars and the tide is with us. We'll reach the island all right.'

It was now possible to make out the small harbour mouth, the broken stone jetty, the chapel ruins on the rocks above. The wind had lessened considerably and the rain had stopped.

It could all have been much worse,

Emma told herself, trying to squash the shiver of fear that had swept over her when she first realised their plight. But although the question was uppermost in her mind, she would not worry Andrew by suggesting to him that though the island might mean a temporary haven, it would not get them home again.

Andrew breathed another small sigh of relief when he found the rowlocks tucked carefully behind the oar blades. Cold hands made him clumsy and it was some minutes before all was in order and he could begin to row. His back was to the land so he was not the first to see the tiny sailing boat moored against the jetty. He was dead tired and his shoulders were aching unbearably when he heard Emma cry out.

'It's them . . . they're here . . . they're safe!'

He rested on the oars and turned to follow her pointing finger. The sight of Yves' little boat brought a vast feeling of relief. He forgot his intense fatigue.

'Thank God for that!' he said. 'I didn't want to worry you, Emma, but I was scared stiff they might have overturned.'

Emma smiled back at him happily.

'I had the same thought,' she admitted. 'Now we know they are safe.'

Andrew started rowing again — this time with renewed energy. The tide was pulling them fast towards the harbour. Once inside, he felt immediately the calmer water but the current beneath the boat was strong and a new fear replaced his earlier worries. Suppose they could not slow the boat down when they reached the jetty? There was no sandy beach ahead on which they could grate to a halt — only a tumble of jagged rocks which would certainly tear the bottom off the boat. Could he, just with oars, arrest their forward momentum? Emma was clutching desperately at the tiller, but he knew she had no experience in handling boats and, anyway, there was little she could do. It was up to him. Tide and wind was sweeping them onward and the jetty was very close.

'Left, Emma, left!' he shouted as it seemed almost certain they would collide with Yves' boat. He had both blades deep in the water now, in an endeavour to control their speed. Emma heard the despair in Andrew's voice and swung the rudder over with every ounce of strength she had. She braced herself for the collision but the boat swung away, veering off towards the shore.

'Keep it left!' Andrew shouted, realising again the danger of the rocks. He hoped the boat might turn a complete circle and give them a second chance to make the jetty. But Emma's strength was draining away.

'I can't, I can't!' she sobbed.

Andrew dropped the oars and moved to help her, but too late. The boat cracked savagely against a jagged rock, tipped sharply to one side, righted itself and was flung forward on the next wave. This time, the rocks claimed their victim. The boat split and its occupants were flung forward with sickening impact.

Emma felt a violent blow on her head. She lay sprawled where the sea had thrown her, the waves washing over her legs, reaching up to her armpits. Only her head lay clear of the water, her face deathly white but for the dark red gash that was sending rivulets of blood down her cheeks and spreading in a widening pool on the wet grey stones around her.

Andrew scrambled clear of the sea and lay for a few moments, gasping. He was bruised from head to foot and soaked to the skin. Tentatively, he felt his limbs — realised that nothing was broken. As his head began to clear and his breath returned to his aching body, he remembered what had happened — remembered Emma. He jumped up, stood unsteadily for a moment or two as dizziness swayed him, and then lurched forward as he caught sight of her lying on the rocks several yards away.

Fear coursed through his body. She was so still! He could see the gash on her face, the blood; knew that she was seriously injured. If only she were not dead!

He all but fell on his knees beside her.

'Emma! Emma! Emma!' he called desperately. But she didn't stir. With an effort of will, fighting the sickness and giddiness he was feeling, Andrew lifted her wrist and groped for her pulse. The knowledge that she was still alive brought a sob of relief.

He reached in his sodden anorak for a handkerchief; wrung the water from it and tried not very successfully to swab the cut on Emma's forehead. She gave a little moan, as if the pain had touched her through her unconsciousness. Andrew sat back, staring at her, wondering what he could do. Like himself, she was soaked to the skin. He could not leave her lying here. She would freeze to death. Yet he knew he hadn't the strength to carry her. Every now and again his head swam in a sickening fashion.

He half pulled, half carried her across the rocks towards the rough scrub grass that lay beyond the fringe of rocks. He was glad that she remained unconscious. At least if he was causing her any pain, she could not feel it. When at last he laid her down, he was near exhaustion point. He knew that he would have to leave her; have to make the effort to go in search of Yves and Julie.

He wasn't sure if he had the strength to do it.

14

Yves looked at Julie's downcast face with a wry smile. They had been here nearly three hours and the novelty had worn off. She was no longer quite so gay.

'Still enjoying your 'fun'?' he asked, but not unkindly.

Julie sighed.

'How is it you always know what I'm really feeling?' she asked. 'You are quite right, of course. It isn't much fun. I'm cold and terribly hungry. I keep thinking about the supper they'll be having soon at the hotel. I wonder if anyone has been worried about us?'

'Almost certainly!' said Yves, walking over to look out of the window for the twentieth time. The rain had stopped but the wind was still blowing quite hard. At least visibility had improved and it might occur to someone to send out a search party. He passed this grain of comfort on to Julie. She looked slightly more cheerful.

'Andrew will be worried if no one else is!' she announced, hugging her knees with her arms.

'I thought you said Andrew was going out in the car somewhere?'

Julie frowned.

'I'd forgotten that. Emma told me just before we left. I asked where to but Emma didn't know. Andrew just said he was going for a drive.' She paused, lost in thought. Then her voice brightened. 'At least Emma knows we were making for the island because I told her. So they'll know where to look if they realise we're in trouble.'

'They are bound to know we are,' Yves commented. 'No one could have sailed a small boat in that storm. I think perhaps I will take a walk down to the harbour to see if anyone is on the way. It will be something to do. You wish to come?'

Julie shivered.

'No, I'm too cold. I'll stay here. At least the bell has stopped ringing. I suppose the wind must have dropped a bit. Isn't it safe to sail back, Yves?'

He shook his head doubtfully.

'I don't think so. I'll have a look in case. The wind's against us and we'd have to tack the whole way. It would be difficult just to get out of the harbour.'

He considered it as he made his way back across the scrub grass to the rocks. In his view, it wasn't worth taking any more risks. Someone would notice their absence sooner or later and send out a boat to pick them up. The worst of the storm was over and it wouldn't be difficult with a motor boat. Even if the worst came to the worst it wouldn't hurt them to spend the night as they were. At least they were dry.

A sudden movement down on the rocks caught his eye. He saw a glint of red — a vague shadowy outline. The light was none too good but his eyesight was keen and he saw that the upright figure was that of a man. So the island was not uninhabited after all.

Cautiously, Yves made his way further down. He was not afraid for himself but he had Julie to think about. He wondered if it could be a hermit, or perhaps a Breton fisherman who lived on the island as a kind of caretaker.

The man seemed to have difficulty in keeping his footing. For a moment Yves wondered if he were drunk. Then he heard a shout, muffled but with a desperate ring to the tone that made the French boy certain it was a call for help.

Throwing caution to the wind, he half ran, half slid across the ground. Then he halted, recognising Andrew and yet not able to believe the evidence of his own eyes.

'Andrew!' he shouted. He cupped his hands to his mouth and shouted again. 'Andrew — here, over here! It is I, Yves Courtelle!'

Andrew turned at the sound of the voice. He was almost afraid to look — afraid in case his ears had misled him. Then he saw Yves and gasped in relief.

'Thank God!' he said under his breath. Yves was hurrying towards him, a look of utter incredulity on his face.

'However did you get here?' he asked, and seeing Andrew's sodden clothing, added with an attempt at humour: 'You swam by the look of it!'

'Motor boat . . . capsized!' Andrew gasped out. 'Emma's on the beach down there — she's hurt.'

Yves wasted no time asking questions. Putting a hand beneath Andrew's elbow to support him, they made their way back to the inert form lying exactly where Andrew had left it.

Both boys bent over Emma. The wound on her forehead was still bleeding but not so badly. The dark lashes lay against her chalk white cheeks. Her breath seemed to them jerky and uneven.

'She hit her head,' Andrew said wretchedly. 'I hope to goodness she hasn't fractured her skull. She's so cold!

I hope . . . ' he broke off, unable to voice his innermost fears. If Emma were to die . . . but it was unthinkable.

'She'll be all right!' Yves said with far more conviction than he felt. 'But we must get her under cover — she'll die of cold out here in those so wet clothes. Do you think you can help me carry her? Julie and I found shelter in a gun emplacement further up.' He pointed to the cliff about them. 'Julie's waiting there now.'

Somehow, between them, with Yves taking most of the weight, they carried Emma up the slope. Andrew was still suffering from shock but when Emma's eyes opened he felt better at once.

'Please put me down. I can walk,' she murmured weakly.

'You have had a bad knock on your head,' Yves told her. 'It is better that we carry you.'

Julie ran out to them when they were still some distance from the shelter.

'What's happened? Who is it?' She broke off as she recognised Andrew. He was deathly white, his clothes clinging to him, his hair wet. He looked half drowned.

'Andrew!' she gasped, shocked by his appearance. 'Whatever has happened?' Then she recognised Emma who gave her a weak smile.

'We came to rescue you and Yves,' Emma said. 'But it looks as if you are rescuing us!'

For once Julie could find nothing to say. Emma's words had struck hard at her conscience. She had guessed Andrew would come to look for them. It was just the kind of foolhardy thing he would do if he thought she was in danger. It made her feel terribly guilty. And Emma, of course, would want to go where Andrew went. Now she had been badly hurt. The blood was still trickling down from her forehead.

A hundred questions flooded her mind but sensibly she withheld them until the boys had put Emma down on the dry floor. Quickly, Julie stripped off her pullover and removing Emma's soaking clothes, helped her into her own dry jersey. Over by the doorway, Yves was lending Andrew his pullover. Then Julie rolled up her anorak to put beneath Emma's head.

'How do you feel?' she asked at last.

'Much better!' Emma said. But she was shivering hard.

Julie went over to Yves. In an undertone, she said:

'We must get back to the hotel, somehow. I'm sure Emma needs a doctor. What *happened*, Andrew?'

Briefly Andrew repeated the story he had just told Yves.

'I'm afraid the boat is a write-off,' he said, his tone so despairing, Julie unthinkingly put her hand on his arm and said:

'It's not your fault, Andrew. I think you were wonderful even to attempt to help us.'

There was no sign of relaxation on Andrew's face. Grimly he said:

'I was an utter fool to try it; even more of a fool not to check the fuel position before we set out. I'll never forgive myself for taking Emma along, either.'

'It wasn't your fault,' Julie insisted, worried by the desperate tone of Andrew's voice and the hard unyielding look in his eyes. 'It was mine . . . I made Yves come here. If I hadn't been so pig-headed none of this would have happened.'

But there was no softening in Andrew's eyes and he seemed oblivious to her attempts to console him. As if she were not there, he turned to Yves and asked:

'Do you think there's any chance at all of sailing back? The wind's dropped to a light breeze. And there's still an hour or two of daylight left.'

Yves nodded.

'The same thought had crossed my mind. I do not see why it should not be done in reasonable safety. It all depends on whether Emma can stand up to the cold. It *will* be cold.'

They all three turned to look at Emma. She was lying with her eyes closed now but at least there was a tinge of colour in her cheeks and the chattering of her teeth had stopped.

Julie went back and knelt down beside her sister.

'How do you feel, Em?'

'A bit of a headache — that's all!'

'You're quite sure? No other pains anywhere?'

'No. I'm all right. Sorry to be such a nuisance.'

Andrew joined them and disregarding Julie, took Emma's hand in his, saying gently:

'Poor little Emma! If only it had been I who got the knock when the boat capsized. I wish to God there was something I could do to help.'

Emma gave a weak smile.

'I'm really quite all right, Andrew. Honestly! And anyway, if it had been you knocked unconscious, however would we have carried you up here. It's much better it should have been me.'

Yves came over to join them.

'If we are going to try it, Andrew, we

should leave at once. It will be dark before long. We cannot delay or it will be too late.'

Emma looked at the French boy questioningly.

'Try what, Yves?'

He explained their plan, telling her it depended upon how *she* felt. They would be perfectly all right here for the night — safe and dry even if they were cold and hungry. No doubt in the morning help would come. But he felt she should have a doctor as soon as possible.

He did not tell her he was sure she was suffering from a slight concussion. He did not wish to alarm her. But he added:

'I think that cut on your forehead needs a stitch. If you feel able to make the journey, then I am sure it is better that we go.'

'We can fix you up somehow so that you can be lying down,' Andrew broke in. 'But it won't be exactly comfortable.'

'If only we had some matches and could get a fire going,' Julie said plaintively. 'We'd be all right here then.'

'After that rain, there would be nothing dry on the island to burn,' Yves said practically. 'Let's waste no more time. The decision is for you, Emma. It depends how badly you are feeling.'

In fact, Emma's head ached intolerably. She wanted nothing more than to be able to close her eyes and keep quite still. But she sensed that both Yves and Andrew wanted to go and although she was too muzzy to reason out why, she did not want to hamper them in any way.

'I'm sure I'll be all right,' she said again.

Andrew gave her hand a squeeze.

'That's my girl!' he said encouragingly.

Julie saw the gesture and heard the affection in Andrew's voice. Although she tried not to think of herself, she could not still the feeling that swept over her . . . part jealousy, part dismay.

She had not really believed, deep down inside, that Andrew had stopped loving her; that he really did prefer Emma. Even finding them in the car together had not shaken her self-confidence; for her intelligence told her that Andrew would never have come running after her if he hadn't wanted to put things right between them. Now the whole situation looked a great deal more serious. For all she knew, her coming to the island with Yves this afternoon might have been the last straw. And Andrew had really turned against her.

'Well, I don't care one way or the other!' she thought. 'I'm not in love with him any more so why should I mind if he's fallen in love with Emma. It's just my pride that's suffering — not my heart!'

But she had no time for further reflection. Yves was shouting to them from the entrance way.

'A boat is coming!' he called. 'A fishing boat. It's coming into the harbour. They must be looking for us.'

He disappeared, racing down to the jetty, aware that this could be their salvation. Whatever happened, he must not allow the boat to depart without them.

'I'd better go, too,' Andrew said, following more slowly. He was still feeling the effects of shock and every now and again, giddiness weakened his head and his legs.

Julie stayed with Emma. Her sister seemed to be asleep and Julie felt a sudden sickening fear. Could she have a more serious injury than they knew about? Was Emma in fact getting weaker all the time? Could she be *dying*?

She stamped on the thought at once. It was melodramatic and hysterical. Of course Emma was all right. It was just the knock on the head making her sleepy.

But as the minutes ticked away, Julie's anxiety grew. Emma seemed completely unaware of what was going on around her. She hadn't even noticed

Yves' or Andrew's departure. Was she really asleep or was she unconscious again?

'Emma?' The name burst from her involuntarily. 'Emma, are you all right?'

'Don't . . . worry . . . fine!' The words were indistinct. 'Andrew? Is . . . Andrew . . . ?'

Julie wasn't sure if Emma knew what she was saying. But the mere fact that she wanted Andrew was enough to make her say:

'You love him, don't you, Emma? You're in love with Andrew.'

'I . . . love . . . Andrew!'

Julie sat back, her hands to her burning cheeks. She couldn't be sure if Emma knew what she had said but she never doubted it was true. She tried to force herself to think only of Emma — lying perhaps desperately ill beside her. Yet her thoughts kept wandering to her own selfish desire to know if Emma and Andrew had really fallen in love.

'I'm horrible!' Julie thought. 'I'm not worth a hair of Emma's head. If I were ill, she wouldn't be thinking about herself; hating me as I'm hating her. But I can't hate my own sister! Emma, forgive me — I'm sorry!'

But at least she could keep her thoughts to herself this time and it was as well, she reflected, as Yves and Andrew came breathlessly into the shelter.

'It's all right, Julie. They've come to find us,' Yves announced cheerfully. 'Two of them are coming up to help carry Emma down to the boat.'

Andrew did not look at Julie. His one over-riding thought was Emma. He dropped on his knees beside her and took her limp cold hand in his own. His face looked desperate with worry.

'Is she unconscious?' he burst out.

'I don't know!' Julie's voice was suddenly weary. There was little doubt in her mind now that Andrew reciprocated Emma's feelings. He could think only of Emma.

Yves came up to Julie and laid his arm across her shoulders.

'Cheer up, Julie!' he said. He was the only one among them who had managed to keep up his spirits. 'I'm sure Emma will be all right!'

Julie turned to him gratefully. She felt like bursting into tears. At least Yves cared how she felt, even if he had mistaken her concern for herself as worry for Emma.

Two Breton fishermen came in through the aperture, their bulky figures in oilskins filling the tiny space. Their faces were brown and weather-beaten, their voices rough as they talked to Yves in a language Julie could not understand. Yves seemed to be directing operations. But for all their size, the men were very gentle as they lifted Emma between them and began the descent to the jetty. Andrew walked beside Emma, his eyes never leaving her face.

Julie walked behind with Yves.

'Apparently your parents and mine raised the alarm when Lindy told them where we'd gone. They guessed Andrew and Emma had come after us when the irate ferryman came storming into the hotel saying the English boy had stolen his boat! We are lucky, I think. It would not have been good for Emma to make that cold journey in my little boat, and I shall be happier when a doctor has seen her.'

Julie walked on silently. She was shivering with cold now that Emma had her warm jersey. Yves took off his anorak and put it over her shoulders. She thought this gesture considerate and typical. He was nice in every way, she reflected — just the sort of boy a girl might fall in love with. Yet she was not in love with him. She'd found him attractive, but as he himself had pointed out, physical attraction and love were two different things. She wondered if he might have taken her more seriously if she'd not been Andrew's fiancée? From the start there'd been a reservation in his manner towards her. It was this which had partly challenged her into taking him more seriously than she might have done if he'd fallen adoringly at her feet! If he realised that she and Andrew were really all washed up, would he behave differently towards her?

But Julie was too cold, tired and dispirited to feel deeply concerned about anything or anyone. Her pride had been bitterly hurt and it would take more than Yves to re-inflate the ego which she had never before lacked. For as far back as she could remember, Andrew had loved her. Other boys, too, had found her attractive and it had always been she, Julie, who broke off the friendships; no boy had ever rejected *her*. Now for the first time in her life, she was learning what it felt like to be turned aside . . . and by Andrew of all people.

With Emma as comfortable as possible and protected from the wind in the boat's tiny wheelhouse, Andrew in attendance at her side, Julie and Yves climbed in and sat down near each other. The fishermen on the jetty cast off and jumped lightly on board. The engine sprang powerfully into life and the sturdy little craft turned to nose its way towards the open sea.

15

Emma lay in bed, her head bandaged, looking like a war victim. Now that the colour had returned to her cheeks, the white bandage suited her.

For the last three days she had felt perfectly well, but the doctor had prescribed a minimum of five days in bed and so she lay, propped up by pillows, feeling a bit of a fraud but enjoying every moment of it — particularly the moments when Andrew was keeping her company. This he did for several hours a day although Emma had repeatedly asked him to go down to the beach with the others.

She nursed her private happiness secretly. No one could ever know what it meant having Andrew so attentive; so tender and affectionate. It was as if he could not do enough to please her. Sometimes he read aloud and she would lie listening to the sound of his voice thinking how much she loved him; how happy she was; how undeserving of all the sympathy the family showered on her for being bed-ridden on their summer holiday.

Emma longed to ask him how things were now between him and Julie but Andrew never mentioned Julie's name and Emma felt it would be too revealing if she were to enquire. She would die of shame if Andrew ever thought she was hoping to replace Julie in his affections.

Julie herself came to Emma's room on frequent but short visits. She did not seem able to sit down and relax for a good long chat the way the rest of the family always did. Her conversation was lively, gay, recounting the plans for the day or the events of the day just past.

Yves seemed to be playing quite a large part in Julie's life, Emma thought. Nearly every sentence included Yves' name and Emma could not help wondering how Andrew felt if Yves and

Julie were always together.

Lindy was the only one who gave her any real information.

'Julie and Andrew are barely on speaking terms. It's both their faults, really. They avoid each other as much as possible. Andrew only has to say he's driving one car for Julie to say she'll go in the other with Yves. And Julie only has to suggest something for everyone to do for Andrew to say he's already planned to do something else. In a way it's quite funny, except that neither of them seems very happy about it.'

Lindy had sighed.

'Of course, Julie's always laughing and gay and she flirts madly with Yves but you know what Yves is like — he sort of side tracks — turns it all into a joke so one never really knows if he likes her or not. He's always terribly polite and pleasant to Andrew but Andrew just glowers at him. It's not surprising, really.'

The younger children told Emma about another search they had all made for the sapphire ring. Mr. Prescott and Andrew had reported the loss to the police but no one had much hope of finding it. Nevertheless, they had had another look in the sand without success. The younger children were obviously enjoying their holiday. Penny had a bucketful of beautiful shells to take home. Paul had his bucket full of shrimps and crabs. The trouble was the crabs ate the shrimps as fast as he could collect them. He was also worried about getting fresh sea water at home. But the worry did not spoil his fun.

Yves, too, came to visit Emma. And the better she got to know him, the better Emma liked him. He alone of the three was happy to talk about their ill-fated island adventure.

'It was fool-hardy of Andrew to take the boat in such too rough conditions,' he said, 'but courageous also. I am afraid he has been in great trouble because of his action.'

'Trouble?' Emma repeated. She felt suddenly guilty. She had done nothing to try to prevent Andrew taking the boat. If she had tried hard enough to dissuade him . . .

'Misfortunately it seems that although the boat was insured, the money the fisherman will receive is not sufficient to buy him a boat of the same condition. Andrew's father has had to offer him quite a large sum to prevent him — how do you say? — to prevent him taking more action against Andrew.'

Emma sighed. Everything looked gloomy once more.

'It was wrong of us — I was with Andrew, don't forget, Yves, so I am also to blame. We were both thinking only of you and Julie and at the time, it seemed the right thing to do.'

'I understand this,' agreed Yves. 'Also I see that neither of you imagined the boat would be wrecked. Andrew feels very bad about it and he has said he will repay every franc his father has had to pay on his behalf. You know, Emma, I think Andrew must love Julie very much.'

'But he has not asked her to get engaged to him again!' The words burst out despite herself.

Yves looked at Emma quizzically.

'That is so. But people have strange ways of showing their love, do you not agree, Emma? For some it is very much on the surface — for others it is all deep down inside.'

'Yes!' Emma agreed in her thoughts. For her it was deep down. That was how she loved Andrew.

As if he had read her thoughts, Yves said:

'And you, Emma — you believe you love Andrew, do you not?'

He saw the quick flush rise to her cheeks and added gently:

'I expect you will think yourself in love many times before it is the real thing. But a first love — that has a very special meaning, I think. One feels it with all one's being. It is only when it is past that one asks oneself how could it have been that way? What was so special about the loved one to cause

281

such great emotion. One cannot really understand oneself in retrospect.'

Still Emma did not reply. She longed to call out:

'But I shall never stop loving Andrew. I could never look back on this time and wonder why I loved him. I'll love him for ever and ever.'

'Love can hurt as well as delight,' Yves went on. 'Once I was very deeply hurt by a young girl for whom I was quite crazy in love!' Emma smiled at his curious English. 'She had no real feeling for me but wished merely to add me to her list of conquests. I vowed I would never fall in love again — and yet it happened — only a few weeks after I'd said goodbye to her, too.'

'Then it can't have been real!' Emma cried. 'If it had been real, it would have lasted in spite of every set-back.'

Yves nodded.

'That is perhaps true, but when one is in love, it always feels like the real thing. I expect you feel your love for Andrew is real, too. But it is very easy to misjudge one's emotions, especially when one is only sixteen.'

'I'm quite old enough to be in love!'

'Yes, indeed! This I do not doubt, but I think you should ask yourself, *chère* Emma, how much of what you feel is just a reflection of Julie. Until she became engaged, Andrew was like a very dear elder brother, was he not? You looked up to him, respected him, liked him very much. But your thoughts did not really become romantic thoughts until your sister's engagement. I think it was then you wished yourself in Julie's shoes — not just because of Andrew himself, but because suddenly her life seemed to have all the romance and glamour and excitement yours did not. Therefore you try to become as much like Julie as possible.'

Emma's face was hot with anger. Suddenly she no longer liked Yves.

'I don't see what right you have to talk like that!' she flared up at him. 'How can you know what I felt — what I feel now? Or what Andrew feels about me. For all you know, he may be falling in love with me. He spends most of the day with me. If he loved Julie so much, why isn't he with her?'

Yves took Emma's hand in his. She tried to withdraw it but he held it fast, stroking the back of her knuckles with his long thin fingers — a strangely soothing gesture.

'I do not want to hurt you, Emma. But it is possible Andrew is so much with you because he feels very guilty about you. It was his fault that you have to lie here in bed instead of enjoying your holiday with the others. He knows it was wrong of him to take you with him that night to the island. He is not normally an irresponsible person but he wanted so much to get to Julie — to stop her spending the night alone with me. He was as much concerned about this, I think, as her physical safety. Therefore he caused you harm — you, the one person who trusted and believed in him implicitly.'

'Then you think his behaviour is the

result of a guilty conscience? That's horrible.'

Yves looked away from the dark, hurt eyes. He had become very fond indeed of Emma — fonder of her than any of the family. He was the last one to wish her hurt and yet he could see all too well behind the façade she chose to show the others. If he had had any right to interfere, he would have pointed out to Andrew that his constant attentions to Emma might be misconstrued by her. Now the only way he, Yves, could prevent her being further hurt was by telling her the truth, no matter how much she hated to hear it.

'I think that's a dis . . . disgusting thing to say!' Emma's voice trembled. She was near to tears. 'I don't believe you!'

Yves still held her hand. He was conscious suddenly of a desire to paint her — her young delicate face so tragic and overflowing with emotion. It was such an expressive face. So much went on within Emma people never saw. But he could see things even she herself did not know. It was true of Julie, too. True of most people in whom he had any interest. He had trained himself from a young age to look behind the facial outlines to the character within. Only by really knowing a person could he paint a true portrait.

'If you really believe I lied, then my words would not distress you!' he pointed out as gently as possible. 'Do not delude yourself, Emma. Andrew is still much in love with Julie. He cannot bear to be with her because he thinks she does not love him. He is also ashamed because his rescue attempt failed and he made more trouble than he hoped to prevent. A man's pride is important to him.'

'Julie sets out to make him look silly!'

'No!' Yves argued. 'She does not really mean to do this. Julie is very young for her age. She acts always on the impulse — first the action, then the thought after it. This sometimes makes her cruel but she is not so intentionally.

You, Emma, will never be young in this way. You are sensitive to the feelings of other people. It is how you are made and you cannot be different any more than Julie can be different.'

Emma knew that Yves had judged Julie correctly. Unwilling though she might be to admit it, she could remember occasions in their childhood when Julie, in a flash of temper, had smashed some favourite toy of Emma's. It was only afterwards, when she saw Emma's distress, that she herself burst into tears, hugging her small sister and begging forgiveness: 'I didn't mean it! I didn't mean to do it!'

But damaging a toy was very different to hurting Andrew. That was much harder to forgive.

Again as if he divined her thoughts, Yves said:

'Julie's treatment of Andrew may not have been very kind but I think it will perhaps turn out a good thing for them both. Andrew was too easy with her. She needs a firm hand — someone to

287

be master of her. Andrew is seeing this now. When he forgives her, he will be different — less yielding with her. And she will respect him more because she realises his love cannot be taken for granted.'

Emma felt a lump in her throat.

'So you think they'll end up . . . ' she paused and then went on bravely . . . 'happily ever after?'

Yves nodded.

'Yes, I do! You should prepare yourself for this, Emma, in case I am right. Do not think too much about Andrew. You know, it would be nice if you would think a little about me instead.'

Emma looked at him startled.

'About *you*? But why? *You* don't need anyone to . . . to think about you.'

Yves laughed.

'Don't I? I am a man just like Andrew. It would be very flattering to me if at least one of the Prescott sisters were to consider me worth a second thought.'

'But Julie . . .'

'No!' Yves broke in, still smiling. 'Julie has no real feeling for me, Emma — only for what I represent. She told me herself that she thought I might be 'fun'. I can understand that a French boy could be a novelty after the English; that she might have the idea I am a little naughty! Julie likes to burn her fingers. But I would like to be liked for myself and it would please me very much if you, Emma, were to say you cared for me just a little.'

'You are not really serious, are you?' Emma asked. Then blushed. 'I mean, you don't really care twopence what I think about you. You're just trying to be kind to me.'

The smile had left Yves' face.

'No, I am not. I am asking *you* to be kind to *me*. I have . . . how do you say in English idiom . . . the weak place in my heart for you, *chère petite* Emma. I would like that we should know one another better. I find you *très sympatique*!'

He had lapsed into a mixture of languages. The desire to say just what he meant — to convince her that he meant it genuinely — made him forget how he spoke the words. He saw the tell-tale colour flood back into Emma's cheeks, and very tenderly, he lifted the hand he still held imprisoned, to his lips.

'You are not angry?' he asked as he replaced it by her side.

Emma was not quite sure how she felt — surprised, touched, but not angry. The surprise was uppermost. It seemed so unbelievable that Yves should be interested in her. She'd been so sure he was attracted to Julie.

'Well, say that you are not cross!' Yves demanded persuasively. 'Tell me in French — not English. This is good for your schooling, too.'

'School!' Emma said on a long sigh. 'What a ghastly thought!'

Yves shook his head.

'No, not ghastly!' he mimicked her accent. 'It is good to learn. I am twenty-two but still I am at school. Tell me what you study, Emma. What is it you wish to be when you leave school?'

Emma hesitated. No one in the whole world knew of her secret ambition to be a writer. No one had read her diaries — kept since her tenth birthday, in which she had written not only her day to day experiences, but poured out her heart. Expressing herself on paper was easier for her than using words.

Slowly, hesitantly, she imparted this to Yves. The French boy did not laugh as she had feared. He nodded and said:

'I can believe you would be a good writer. You feel. It is necessary to feel if you are to write just as if you are to paint. One must know about life if one wishes to describe it in paint or in ink. Would you write to me when you returned to England, Emma? It would make me very happy.'

Again Emma found herself blushing. She had never had a pen-friend like some of the girls at school. Julie had

291

written to a girl in Hong Kong and to a boy in America throughout her teens. But somehow Emma had never felt she could communicate with a stranger. But with Yves . . . he was not a stranger. He knew too much about her. It would be nice to have someone in whom she could confide.

'Think about it and tell me another time,' Yves broke in on her thoughts. 'Fortunately, you do not leave for five more days. Tomorrow you will be allowed up, no? We must arrange something to celebrate the occasion. But not that you become tired.'

When he had gone, Emma lay back on the pillows, her eyes closed. While Yves had remained in the room with her, his soft French voice strangely lulling, comforting, she had not felt the full impact of what he had said. Only now did she face up to what he had told her — that Andrew wasn't in the least in love with her; that he still loved Julie . . . and Julie loved him.

'It's what I want for Andrew!' she

told herself. But suddenly she realised that she wasn't really so unselfish as she had made herself out to be. She had been secretly nursing the hope that Andrew would turn to her for comfort — just as he had done that night on the beach. She had *wanted* things to go wrong between him and Julie; she had wanted to take what was rightfully Julie's from her.

Her cheeks flushed and she bit her lip to stop the trembling. She had lied to herself; made herself believe that she wanted Andrew's happiness more than her own. But the truth was she had been happiest herself when he was unhappy. These last few days she had lived in a rosy cloud of contentment; knowing Andrew was not with Julie; telling herself he preferred to be with her!

And Yves had seen the truth.

She covered her burning cheeks with her hands. She felt deeply ashamed. Yves had said she had not started to think about Andrew romantically until

Julie's engagement. Was it true? Her diary would tell her, but she knew, without opening the little book, that it was on the night of Julie's twenty-first party that she had first written those words: *I love Andrew!* And if Yves were right about this, then he could be right about her wanting to be in Julie's shoes, the centre of attraction instead of on the fringe.

'But I do love Andrew!' she whispered the words out loud. 'I do. I've always loved him.'

She tried to conjure up the image of his face; to imagine the particular timbre of his voice; to re-live the memory of that one strange kiss. But suddenly it was as if her mind were a void. She could think of nothing but her own deep shame.

16

Andrew said:

'It's lovely to have you back with us, Emma!'

It was a beautiful day and everyone, including Yves' parents, was down on the beach. The younger children were splashing about in the sparkling water, the older generation sitting comfortably in deck chairs by the sand dunes. Yves, Julie, Andrew and Emma had settled down on beach towels, sunbathing. Until Andrew spoke conversation had been desultory. With one brief sentence, he had brought it back to a personal level.

Emma blushed. Julie, watching her sister's tell-tale face, clenched her hands at her sides.

'You make it sound as if Emma had been round the world!' she said in a small, hard voice.

The colour in Emma's cheeks deepened. Yves tried tactfully to lessen the tension that suddenly held them all in its grip.

'Five days can seem quite a long time when you are lying in bed!' he said in his soft French voice. 'I think it is fortunate we have so nice a hot, sunny day for Emma to return to the beach.'

Grateful for the opening, Emma said brightly:

'Yes, it is lovely. Do you know the last time I was down here was on the Thursday — the day . . . ' She broke off, wishing she could have bitten off her own tongue.

'The day I chucked my engagement ring away!'

Julie's voice was cold and violent. Now it was Andrew who coloured.

'That was an idiotic thing to say!' he retorted.

'No more idiotic than you thinking it!' said Julie ambiguously. 'Don't deny you thought I'd been careless.'

'I'm not denying it. If you'd valued it

at all, you would have been more careful.'

'Please! Please don't quarrel!' Emma's small voice, charged with distress, focussed both Julie's and Andrew's attention on her.

This time, Julie made no effort to control herself.

'A fat lot you care if we quarrel!' she cried, jumping to her feet and staring down at Emma accusingly. 'It suits you very well and don't try to pretend otherwise.'

'Julie!' Both boys spoke her name, instantaneous in their disapproval.

'You've gone too far,' Andrew cried, also getting on his feet his face white and stern. 'Emma has nothing to do with our quarrel or the lost ring or anything else. You're not going to put the blame on her.'

'That's right — protect her at all costs. Don't bother about my feelings.' Suddenly Julie's eyes were brimming with tears. She caught her trembling lower lip between small white teeth and clenched her fists at her sides. 'I hate you, Andrew,' she cried. 'I *hate* you!'

She swung round and started to walk away from them. Andrew stood staring after her, a strange look of bewilderment on his face.

'I don't understand. I just *don't* understand!' he muttered. Yves sighed.

'It is quite simple, Andrew. Julie is jealous of Emma. She's in love with you — that's all.'

Andrew drew in his breath sharply. He seemed about to begin an argument with Yves but changed his mind and walked off, his pace quickening to a run as he followed Julie.

Yves lay back on his towel, sighing.

'At least he is beginning to understand,' he said, more to himself than to Emma. 'Now, perhaps, they will be happy.'

Emma, too, lay back, closing her eyes against the bright glare of the sun. The last few minutes had been emotionally deeply upsetting for her. Her nerves were completely on edge. Andrew wasn't the only one who was beginning to understand that Julie loved him. Emma, too, could see that 'I hate you' might just as well mean 'I love you'. She rolled over on her side and looked at Yves with an appeal in her eyes.

'I never wanted Julie to be unhappy. I thought she didn't love him. Really and truly, Yves!'

He opened his eyes and smiled at her.

'I know. Julie will realise it too, once she can think about anything but her own unhappiness. You and your sister will be friends again, believe me.'

'Will we?' Emma's voice was wistful. 'I've always loved Julie. I always admired her, wished I was like her. I couldn't bear it if she went on hating me.'

Yves laid a hand gently on Emma's warm forearm.

'She doesn't hate you, Emma. You will be even better friends after this is over. But it will be different. You won't be the elder and the younger one any more but equal — two women who can talk to each other and be very close in a grown-up way. I don't think you will want to be like Julie any more. You will prefer, as I do, that you should be yourself.'

Emma felt the comfort of his words quieten her mind just as the touch of his hand on her arm soothed the tension that was purely physical.

'You are always so kind and understanding, Yves. Much more so than Andrew . . . ' She broke off, seeing the laughter in Yves' eyes. 'What's so funny?' she asked in a more normal voice.

'I never thought to hear you, *petite* Emma, speak of Andrew as anything but perfect.'

The colour rose as swiftly as always to Emma's cheeks, but this time she could smile, too.

'Oh, well, I suppose I always knew in my heart that he wasn't *perfect* — human beings never are, are they? I just didn't look for his faults. I suppose he has been a bit weak with Julie. I mean, if he'd stood up for himself at the beginning of the holiday, none of this would have happened, would it?'

'I think he will be different now. He has learned a lot these last ten days. I, too, have learned a great deal. I have learned to become most deeply fond of you, Emma. I know you are very young still in years but I would like to think that I shall still know you when you are older. Will your parents allow me to come and visit you in England, do you think?'

'Visit *me*?' Emma gasped out the words.

'Why not? And who else if not you? You did not think *I* was falling in love with Julie, did you? If I have fallen a little in love with anyone, it is with you, Emma. One day that little could become a great deal.'

Emma was staring at her companion, her eyes still wide with surprise and confusion. It seemed so improbable that any boy could really be in love with her. It was always Julie the boys admired. Here, totally unexpectedly, was one boy who liked her better than Julie; who liked her for herself.

And Yves, how did she feel about him? She wasn't sure. Everything was very confusing. She had been quite certain about her love for Andrew; and thought it would last all her life. If her emotions were so unreliable, how could she possibly trust herself to judge her feelings towards anyone?

Yves' eyes were still full of laughter.

'You look so sweet and solemn and so like a little girl who is quite, quite lost. Don't worry so much, Emma. Life is to be enjoyed happily. You must not make of it a torment. Forget what I said. We will be friends — very good friends, no?'

'But I don't know if I want to forget it!' Emma cried impulsively.

This time Yves did not laugh.

'That is the most charming thing you have said to me. It gives me much hope for the future. We shall write to each other, no? As we said the other day? This way we will get to know each other very well during the time you are finishing growing up.'

It was on the tip of Emma's tongue to argue that she was grown-up, but if nothing else, this holiday had served one purpose — it had shown her just how incapable she was of coping with adult life. She didn't want the complications of love — only the excitement and pleasures. Remembering, she knew that she had not really enjoyed Andrew's kisses. They had frightened and upset her. With Yves, everything was so much less complicated. He seemed to understand her needs, her thoughts. She wondered how he had sensed that she wasn't ready yet to fall in love with him but that she wanted him as a dear and close friend.

'I wonder if he will always understand me!' Emma thought. As if by way of reply, his hand reached out for hers and held it firmly, reassuringly. 'I wonder if we will meet again after this holiday! If I'll still know him when I'm Julie's age. It would be nice if he could come to my twenty-first birthday party. I'd have a new dress and . . . '

She was woken abruptly from her reverie by the shouting of the children as they came racing across the sand towards her. Lindy was with them and Emma could see her friend waving frantically but they were all talking at once so it was impossible to hear what they were saying.

She and Yves waited until three hot and panting bodies flung themselves down in the sand.

'We've found it!'

'We've got the ring — Julie's ring!'

'Penny had it all the time!'

'We've found it. We've found it!'

There, in Penny's hot sandy little fist, lay Julie's sapphire ring.

'But where?' Emma gasped out.

'Isn't it wonderful?' Lindy's face was wreathed in smiles. 'And so silly, really. Just nobody thought of looking *there*!'

'If one of you does not soon tell me

where you found it, I shall go a little crazy!' said Yves, shaking Paul's shoulder impatiently.

'It was in my bucket!' said Penny. 'With my shells. I don't know how it got there. I didn't *put* it there.'

'But there it was!' Lindy finished. 'Penny wanted to wash her shells because they were all sandy, so we tipped them into a shallow pool of water and we were putting them back one by one and there it was. Isn't it wonderful? Where's Julie? And Andrew? We must tell them. Let's go and tell Mother and the others.'

They raced off in a hot, excited bunch.

Emma let out her breath.

'I still can't quite believe it!' she said. 'I *am* glad. I suppose it could have dropped into the bucket if someone shook out Julie's towel. It seems a bit coincidental but I can't see how else it got there.'

'It hasn't much importance,' said Yves. 'Though I think little Penny might have scooped it up with her hands, thinking it was one of those little pieces of coloured glass washed smooth by the sea which she greatly treasures. Anyway, it is found. Do you know, Emma, I have never yet prayed to St. Anthony and not found what I have looked for. Once when I was quite a small boy, my mother was walking home with me along a wide street. It was winter and there was thick snow on the ground. It was nearly dark and the street lamps were lit. When we reached home my mother found she had lost one of her pearl ear-rings. Well, we prayed to St. Anthony and we went back to look for it. And we found it — lying in the snow — one tiny pearl in all that snow. It could have been anywhere along that road, trodden in, picked up by passers-by. But it lay beneath a lamp, shining. Since then, I have never doubted.'

'And you prayed for Julie's ring to be found?'

Yves nodded, smiling.

Emma gave a deep sigh.

'It's like a fairy story, a true one,' she said. 'I can't wait to see Julie's face — and Andrew's.'

★ ★ ★

Emma was tired. In a few minutes, she would go upstairs to bed but just for a moment longer she wanted to remain on the stairs where she was sitting, savouring her happiness. The evening had been like a repetition of Julie's party. Julie and Andrew were engaged again. Mr. Prescott had made a kind of game about the lost ring and without realising that Andrew and Julie had really broken off their engagement, insisted that they go through the formalities of becoming engaged again. Andrew must give Julie the ring, put it on her finger and kiss her in front of everyone. He would make another speech, wishing them happiness.

Somehow, no one had thought the idea silly and everyone, even the other hotel guests, had drunk champagne and toasted the 'happy couple' and wished them well. And Julie had been as radiant as she was on the other night, her eyes like stars, her hand clasped tightly in Andrew's. They did not leave each other's side and no one could have doubted their love for each other.

Suddenly, the door of the salon burst open and Emma was no longer alone. It was Julie, standing at the foot of the stairs saying:

'Emma? I wondered where you were? Are you all right, darling? What are you doing out here alone?'

Her voice was full of warmth, as was the arm she put round Emma's shoulders.

'I'm perfectly all right, Julie. I've just been up to take the children some of those petit fours Madame was offering round. As I came downstairs, I suddenly felt so happy I just sat down to enjoy it. I'm so glad everything has turned out right, Julie.'

Julie's squeezed Emma's hand.

'I'm happy, too, completely happy now I know you are. I said some horrible things to you, Emma. Can you ever forgive me? I didn't mean them, you know. It was just that I was so miserable and . . . '

'Yes, I know. I've forgotten them!'

'You are sweet, Emma. I'm lucky to have you for a sister. It's one of the reasons I was so jealous — I could see for myself why Andrew preferred you to me.'

'But, Julie, he didn't . . . '

'Well even if he didn't, he had every reason to do so. I told him so, too. But I'm going to be different from now on, Em. You see! I'll just never say an unkind word to anyone, ever again.'

'Oh, Julie!' Emma laughed. Julie laughed, too.

'All right, I know I'll never be able to live up to that standard but I'm going to try. Coming back, Emma?'

'In a minute. You know I like being alone.'

Julie nodded. With a last fond look at

her sister, she ran gaily back to the salon.

But Emma was not to remain alone. Yves came out and sat beside her. But somehow he did not impinge on her solitude but became part of the moment, just as their two bodies were merged into the increasing darkness of the hallway.

'Happy?'

'Oh, yes!' Emma breathed.

'And I, too. If I am at all unhappy, it is only because the day after tomorrow, you will all be gone.'

'Well, yes!' Emma's voice was dreamy as it became when she was deep in thought. 'But I don't think we will be altogether gone. I mean ... ' she struggled for the right words ... 'I think I'm trying to say that people always leave little bits of themselves in the places they go — just a whisper of themselves. You can feel it in empty houses — a kind of atmosphere that I believe comes from the tiny fragments each person leaves when they go.'

'Emma, will you leave more than just a whisper for me? Will you leave me a happy memory, too?'

His face was very near to hers in the darkness. The colour rushed to her cheeks. Yves was drawing her towards him.

'Cripes!' said a voice from above. 'He's going to kiss her!'

'Paul! Penny!' Emma gasped, outraged that they had been eavesdropping from the landing above; cross with herself because she had not guessed, as she should have done, that they would be there.

But Yves was laughing.

'You are quite right!' he called back to them. 'If you watch very carefully, you will see how it is done.'

But he knew and Emma knew that the darkness was complete and as his lips touched hers and lay there softly for a moment, the kiss was theirs alone.

'Pooh!' said an indignant voice from above. 'That's not fair. We can't see!'

Other titles in the
Linford Romance Library:

TWISTED TAPESTRIES

Joyce Johnson

Jenna Pascoe is a Cornish fisherman's daughter. When her parents receive news that her mother's sister, aunt Olive, is coming home to England from Italy, they refuse to acknowledge her. Family secrets resurface and Jenna's initial delight turns to dismay. However, Olive and her family turn up at their home, and Jenna meets her handsome cousin Allesandro. How will the families resolve their differences — and how will cousins, Jenna and Allesandro cope with their growing feelings for each other . . . ?

A STRANGER'S LOVE

Valerie Holmes

Megan has good reason to hate the prosperous Ackton family, the mill owners whom she holds responsible for her mother's death. However, determined that they will not shorten her life, she runs away. After falling into a canal, she is accused of being a madwoman for attempting suicide, and is sent to the asylum. Megan is rescued from her fate by Mr Nathan Ackton, and finds that she owes her liberty to a member of the family she loathes.